BLACK FANG

II

MIRIKA MAYO CORNELIUS

BLACK FANG

Copyright © Mirika Mayo Cornelius, August 2025
ISBN: 978-1-946870-21-6

An Akirim Press Publishing
Book Cover by Mirika Mayo Cornelius
www.akirimpress.com

Acknowledgements

To God be the glory. He allows me to share this story. Bless the Father, the Son Jesus and the Holy Ghost.

Thanks to all who have supported me in my family and beyond.

Dedication

This story is dedicated to my son.

BLACK FANG

After everything in her life crumbles, Bailey finally enters Tylon to find the answers to her life that she's been searching for, but while there, she inherits even more enemies than she's bargained for and they want the ultimate revenge.

As a result of the mounting pressure, Bailey finally embraces her full potential and power being of a Tylonthian father and a courageous mother, but that power backfires, leading her to more destruction as her fangs take the life of someone else that she will forever live to regret.

Table of Contents

Chapter One

Eric steps from his house and onto the porch with a visibly upset Bailey. Her brown, bright eyes are bloodshot from so much crying at her late friend's funeral, and the guilt from the inescapable murder burdens her soul. Her throat visibly shakes as she asks once more.

"Take me to Tylon."

"Step down here with me, Bailey," he requests, uneasy about anyone else hearing their conversation. She does what he requests, and as she steps down, Eric holds her hand in efforts to comfort her. He can tell that each move she makes creates an internal devastation that he can't and has never felt before. To a Ty, a win is a win, and he's very aware that it isn't at all quite like that with a duel heritage.

"I really need to leave. I need to get out of here. I can't stay."

"Listen, Bailey, please. I know all of this is far too much for you to..."

"Who's at the door?" his guardian shouts from inside the house, so Eric quickly releases Bailey's hand, runs back up to the door and puts the woman of the house at ease.

"It's just a friend of mine. I'll be back," he replies, shutting the front door back and returning to Bailey so they can take a long walk down the street. "Bailey, I can't take you to Tylon."

"I'm of Tylon. That's what you said. That's what you and my dad told me."

"Have you seen him?"

"No. He hasn't even checked on me. He sees what happened, and he just abandoned me, again!"

"No, it's not like that. He can't be around all the time visibly is all. He'll be around. Trust me, but I can't take you to Tylon."

"Why not? I can't stay here. I have to leave," she cries softly. "I keep dreaming of what happened, and I see her all the time. I feel like a murderer, Eric. I killed my best friend, and I didn't even have a choice. I don't feel human anymore. I feel like some out of control monster."

Eric, instead of taking her on a long walk, decides to talk to her at the side of the brick house beneath his bedroom window. "I understand, Bailey. I was there, too, remember? I know this is one of the most traumatizing years for you, and I honestly wish things didn't have to end up this way. I prefer it though." He takes her by both her hands and earnestly states, "You father was right. You have to believe him. He didn't lie to you about any of this. Delight hated you. You heard her and saw her come to kill you. It was self-defense."

"It wasn't her fault."

"Well if you can't find fault in her, then there should be no reason you should find fault in yourself. You did everything you could, and you're not a monster. You're still yourself, except you have inherited some qualities that will keep you connected to your father forever and also keep you alive. He's a descent, upstanding man, but as far as Tylon, if I go back, I'm in trouble. That's why I can't take you."

"With your parents?"

"Yeah, and I'll probably be assigned a mission. Plus, no one like you has ever been to Tylon. I don't even know if you can actually get back to this side, and then there's your mom. You have to think about her, and it's just too much. It's too much that I've never done or even thought about doing."

"This is too much for me, Eric. Please, I need to go to Tylon."

"Why? What will going to Tylon solve?"

"Everything." Her teary eyes meet his, and they explain everything else to him.

"You need to meet your family, don't you?"

"Yes. I need to know who I truly am and why. I'm lost, Eric, and what if my mom ever finds out. I'm going to have to explain. He'd always told us that he didn't have any more family since the fire, and now I know that was a total lie. My mom is devastated and hurt, but if she still knew he was alive, that the images of him she sees at times before her eyes are actually real, it may soothe her heart, as it did mine."

Eric takes a deep breath, closes his eyes for a while as they stand there in silence, and finally gives in. "I'll come by your window tonight and we'll leave from there. The earlier we leave the sooner we can get back, if we can get back." He glances down at her. "I'll take you, Bailey. I'll take you."

"Thank you."

"Let me walk you back home."

Chapter Two

Bailey's mother hasn't been in the bed for more than thirty minutes yet, so it's evident to Bailey that she's nowhere near fast asleep. Pacing around her bedroom in the dark, she reviews everything her father told her while also preparing a greeting for a family that's never even heard of her. Suddenly, she stops pacing and wonders, what if they *have* heard of her? What if her and her mother are the ones that don't know anything about everything and everyone else is fully aware of everything?

As she rehearses all that she will say and how she will stand, tall and confidently, like a superhero, she wonders if she should alert everyone to the fang in her chest that she desperately and successfully has hidden from her mom. With a fitting shirt, one can almost see the outline of the fang, but she doesn't want to wear a super loose fitting shirt either because she wants to look tidy, put together and not just appear like she came to lounge around.

She looks in her mirror and inspects her clothing, but then stops. "Should I wear sandals?" Suddenly, there's a knock on the bedroom window, and she immediately knows who it is. She goes to the curtain, shoves the blinds up and there Eric stands. Then she mouths, "But I don't think my mom is asleep."

He mouths back, "Open the window," and when she does he continues, "Well, go see. You act like you don't have the speed to do it without her knowing or something," he groans when he decodes the pitiful look on her face. "You want me to check real quick?"

"No, no, just..." she says looking back toward her bedroom door, "Wait right here. I'll go check, and if she's not, I definitely won't come back because she'll be asking me why I'm fully dressed like I'm going out somewhere in the middle of the night."

"Well, she wouldn't be wrong. This is your crazy idea," he responds and before he turns back to face her, she's already out of the bedroom and in the hallway. In about ten more seconds, she's climbing out of the window, and they're both heading into her backyard. She grabs his wrist, not understanding why he's headed back there."

"I figure this is close enough to get you back home safely and in one piece. What? You thought we were leaving from my house?"

"Well, anywhere but here. Does it have to be here?"

"It doesn't have to be, but just in case we're late getting back. I'm honestly not sure if we will come back to this same exact spot, but I'd rather have the odds on our side than not."

"So you don't know?"

"Bailey, since I left, I haven't been back home, so it's not like I do this every single day. I do know my way back home, but I just don't know how everything else goes, especially with you. Like what if you get trapped or something?"

"Trapped? What do you mean trapped?"

"Like trapped in the thing. I don't know what it's called. The thing."

"What thing? Trapped as in I can't get out?" she asks hysterically.

14

"That is what trapped means, but I'm thinking I would be able to get you out somehow."

"But what makes you think I will get trapped and not you?"

"Because you're half me, and you might just go half the way," he roars laughing, gripping his stomach. "And then I might have to throw you a beam," he chuckles, "and yank you the rest of the way."

"That's not funny, Eric! You scared me. You are playing right?"

"I dunno. Am I?" he asks as they reach the backyard, moving toward the big, beautiful tree in the yard with roots that crawl the surface of the ground. Then he gently takes her by the hand, guiding her closer to him. "Now I need you to stand as close as you can to me, look into my eyes and don't turn away, no matter what. Find me and I'll find you. I won't let you go, Bailey. I won't let you go."

"Don't. I'm scared."

"I got you." He takes a deep breath, before saying, "Okay, let's go." In the next second, he says, "We're here."

"We're what?" she asks, snapping out of her gaze into his eyes because he's already ended his. "That's it?"

"Eric!" shouts an unknown lady's voice.

"Ma, I can explain."

Completely lost on what's happening, Bailey stands there in shock that she's been warped directly in the middle of what looks to be dinner at Eric's actual parents' other dimensional house. The absolutely gorgeous woman, eating something orange in color that's not carrots, candied yams or an orange, continues slicing before stabbing it with her fingernail, putting it inside her mouth and addressing Eric once again.

"No you can't. You left here for so long, and you didn't so much as visit. I knew you were over there somewhere, and no one knew how you got out. Hanging out with the other side. I knew it. It's just like I told you, Joe!"

"And who is this?" asks his perfectly sculpted father.

Bailey nearly leaps from her skin, but Eric holds her hand tighter as he scolds his dad with his eyes for sneaking up on her like that. He stands two feet behind her, and his voice is so deep and loud that she even felt it through her chest.

"This is Bailey. She's my uh... girlfriend, and she's one of us, a Ty."

"No she isn't. I've never seen her before a day in my life, and I know everyone's children. Whose child is she?" Eric's mom asks.

"Her dad is..."

"It's nice to meet you, Mrs..."

"Excuse me?" Eric's mom interjects stunned and highly offended.

"I forgot to tell you not to call anyone here Mr. or Mrs. It's disrespectful."

"What? Why didn't you tell me?" Bailey panics.

"So you're from the other side," she asks standing up from the table and walking over to where Bailey stands. Eric feels her hand trembling, so he holds it tighter to make her understand that he is there and not leaving her. They both watch as his mom looks her over closely for at least one full minute, then she stops. "Yjotar's daughter, a half-blood. Am I right?"

"Yjotar? Are you sure, Clivvanna?" Joe asks, his real name being Joevahn.

"Positive." She shoots a glance at Eric. "Aren't I right, runaway baby boy?"

He nods and shakes his head. "This is Bailey. We've been friends since I can remember my time on the other side, and she needed to come here because..."

"Her father left us, and he left us twice. I know, and I'm sorry you had to feel that, Bailey. What I don't know is why you left, Eric. Sit and eat. I've had to prepare your plate for years, and now you show up. You know I cook for you every day, and you didn't even bother to show up for dinner."

"Come on, Bailey, you can sit and down and have some?"

"No thank you." Bailey wants to vomit at the sight of what looks like raw meat and moving cantaloupe, but when Eric taps her foot, she quickly changes her mind. "Well, I will except I don't know what..."

"This is meat. This is vegetable. This is fruit. This is starch..." his mother explains while pointing her fingernail at each item on her plate.

"We don't call the food by the food name here, Bailey, so she isn't being mean or anything."

"Yes, yes, okay, well, I'll eat the fruit."

"Good. Delicious." Eric's mother leans over and places bowl of fruit in front of Bailey. "Dig in. And now back to you, son. Explain."

"Mom, I didn't want to do the whole rite of passage. I still don't. It's not necessary. Besides, I already did something that counts toward it anyway, so we're even. I'm a man."

"You mean you did what already? Joe, pass the whites."

"Salt, mom. We have company."

"Salt," she corrects herself. "Pass the white salt."

"Not white salt, mom. Just salt."

"Salt. Pass the salt, Joe."

Bailey stares. It's all she can do is stare, and she stares so much that Eric's parents stop eating and stare back at her which springs her into speaking, clearing up what Eric failed to clear up.

"Eric saved my life." As soon as she says it, they both look at him and Eric drops his head as if Bailey said the wrong thing.

"Yes, I saved her life, but she couldn't and wouldn't have been able to do it on her own. I had to step in, so it's legit. She handled it on her own. I had to put my life on the line," he pauses, "for hers, and I wouldn't change a thing."

"Who did you save her from?"

"Xidon's daughter."

Everything stops. His mother looks at his father, and then they both look at Eric. "Don't mention his name again in this space. I didn't know he had a daughter. She went with him?"

"No. She's hybrid, like Bailey, and now you see why I had to assist. They, her and Bailey," he says for clarification, "were best friends. Bailey wasn't ready. She loved her, too much, so I had to step in…"

"Don't say anymore," she commands as tears well up in her eyes. "As long as you're okay. Excuse me." She stands and walks into another area of the circular, dome-like house that appears to be translucent from the outside, but everyone inside can see outside. People are walking by and not one person yet has glanced in.

"Son, tell me the truth. How bad were you hurt during this unauthorized mission?" his dad asks.

"Here," he says pointing to his injury. "What's wrong with Mom? I succeeded. I'm here. You would've known immediately if something permanent happened to me and nothing did."

"Something did happen to you, Ericon," he responds as Bailey rapidly glances at Eric thinking to herself, Ericon? "You may not have known, but something did happen, and it happened to me at the same time it was happening to you."

"What?" Eric asks confused. "Dad," he stutters, "what do you mean something happened to you? Are you okay?" Grief and worry overtake Eric's face as if he is finally aware that something terrible possibly went wrong.

"Yes, yes. I'm fine. Now, I'm fine. Your mother, don't worry about her. She will be okay as well because this is all hitting her as if I lied."

"Lied? Lied about what?"

"Well, she thought I lied. She always thought that she would have the most heightened connection with you, however, it turns out that she didn't know you were near death."

"What do you mean? I was never..." he quickly states, looking over at Bailey and slightly shaking his head before taking his attention back to his father.

"Yes, you were. You nearly gave your life for her, Ericon. The reason I know is because at the moment you were dying, my strength left to you. It was just a little bit, and it's a strength I can't retrieve. The only person it could have gone to is you, to keep you alive."

"It was more than just a little bit, Joe." Eric's mom returns. "Don't lie to him, just like you didn't lie to me. I thought you did, but you didn't. I made myself believe you lied to me, and I'm sorry, Joe. Eric," she continues, turning to him. "You father gave about half his power to you that day. It's his duty. Son, the reason why you probably didn't feel yourself slipping is because..."

"Because I released it. I didn't fight it. I knew it was you. We hadn't seen you in so long, so I knew you were there deep in myself, I knew," says his father, "and I needed you to return home. I would have let you have all of it. It was painful, but it was worth it. You're here now. I would have given you all my power and strength and dropped dead myself before I allowed you to perish. Son, your power isn't as great there as it is here because you aren't like her. You aren't a dual breed. Xidon's daughter almost killed you. I never thought you would leave like that so I never told you because you weren't old enough, but never battle on another's grounds. Never."

Tears flow from Eric's eyes as he listens to his father, his life saver, the family who he left for what he knows as silly reasons to them. Feeling a deep sense of remorse, he goes to hug his father, and they leave and walk into another room, leaving Bailey alone with his mother.

Uneasy, Bailey puts her fork down, places her hands beneath the table and as she notices the tears in Clivvanna's eyes, she utters the words, "I'm sorry. I didn't want him to do it, but he insisted that I would have been killed."

"I understand. I want to talk to you. Come sit with me."

They both walk towards the other room and sit down. Bailey is nervous and doesn't like to be away from Eric, but she calms herself down, fighting the intrusive thoughts that are bombarding her that something is going to go terribly wrong during this visit. The feeling is overwhelming, but she's kept it to herself. The last thing she wants to do is make the family feel like she's afraid of them.

They both sit down on two cream high back chairs, Clivvanna on one side of the room and Bailey on the other, making her feel extremely isolated. Clivvanna stares for about one full minute before speaking.

"Bailey, your father is a treasure. Yjotar is one of those who will live forever in the hearts of our people. He's magnificent and capable, even in death, as you well know. Whenever us parents leave this earth, we are responsible for passing on an inheritance in full, meaning ourselves. What disturbed me, Bailey, is that Eric's inheritance had to be given early and no one can know. Absolutely no one. It will make Joe a target for any enemy. I didn't believe him when it happened, but it all makes sense now. I lost nothing. Johvahn, my dear husband, he lost so much, but now that Eric is back, I need you to know that he must stay. Do you understand?"

Bailey sits there not knowing how to respond or even if she should. The tone of Clivvanna's voice was soft yet stern, and a hopelessness creeps across Bailey's body with the conclusion of the question.

"This doesn't mean that he can't take you back home, but don't expect him to remain there with you. His nearly giving his life for you, took much of my husband's life, his father's life, and you, Bailey, owe us him. I am aware of your bond now, but our bond as a family, is greater. You will return to your mother, and you will never return here again. I'm glad you are alive, and Yjotar, this is for the best," she continues, aware that he may be listening. "Her mother needs her at home," she states, staring through Bailey.

"What if he doesn't return after taking me, even if I ask him to return?" she asks as tears roll down her face.

"There's no need to cry, Bailey. He will return. He has his father's strength now which has left us vulnerable. This is a vulnerability that we have kept secret since you killed..."

"My best friend, Delight."

"Yes, killed her, not on purpose, but out of necessity. I'm aware. You wouldn't want anyone to come and kill us, Eric's parents would you because there has already been damage done to us, now would you?"

"Why would anyone want to hurt you?"

"The same reason Delight wanted to kill you. Here in Tylon, Bailey, there are no fights to see another visible day. There are only fights to win permanently. Anything can happen and that will lead to battle, some of those battles are long, like your father's. Other's are quick, like yours. Some come from the past. That's why we need Eric here. Security measures."

"Not love?"

"I love him more than you know. Would you like to test it?" she snaps back at Bailey.

"Test what, mom?" Eric asks as he sits on the chair. Bailey doesn't see him walk in because he used his powers again. His powers are much faster here than on the other side.

"Her cooking. There's no reason why we have her here and don't at least test some of the food from her side. What dishes do you make?"

"Ma," Eric asks suspiciously at both her and Bailey, noticing, Bailey quickly wiping her face. "What kinda conversation is this? Bailey, she didn't come here to cook, and she has to get back home soon. I brought her here to introduce her to the place and..."

"My family. I would like to meet my family before I go back home if that's something that I can actually do."

"Yeah, yeah that's something we can do. Ma, will you?"

"Certainly. Don't cry, Bailey. I understand the connection that you have with your father. It's the same connection that I have with my son. You want him with you, and since he has changed, you need more of him around in family, a family that you've never known. Come with us. We'll go."

"Good, come on, Bailey." He stands and approaches her while whispering, "Are you good?"

"Yeah, yeah... it's just a lot. I'm having a bunch of emotions."

Eric then takes her by the hand. "Come on. Let's go. My mom will introduce you to the family so that it will go over smoother than if I take you alone."

Chapter Three

The air, as soon as Bailey steps outside, gives her a rush with each breath she takes, and she looks over at Eric in amazement. Her body immediately feels lighter and cooler than before.

"Eric? What's going on with me? Am I dying?"

He laughs, "Dying? You look alive to me."

"No really, every time I take a breath, I feel like..."

"It's your body growing accustomed to this side. It will go away soon. You should've felt it as soon as you got here, but since you were inside, I'm assuming that the atmosphere wasn't as potent," Clivvanna interrupts. "How did you feel, Eric, when you got to her side?"

Eric, annoyed by the question because he knows she's trying to make him feel terrible for leaving and not returning. "I felt fine. Just fine. I adjusted well."

"Not too well I see. You're looking better already since you've been back home, doesn't he, Bailey. It looks like he never should have left."

As she walks down the walkway beside Eric, she doesn't even look up at Eric because she knows why she's saying all of what she's saying. It's a reminder that Eric belongs at home, and Bailey truly believes that she will face the wrath of his assumingly powerful mother if she doesn't help that happen.

After walking for a while, she notices that no one here has cars, and there are no real streets. No matter where she looks, there is no transportation, and no one seems to care because instead of streets for automobiles, she notices they are on one side of the pathway and faster people are on the other side. It's like a three lane walkway. No one is in the furthest lane.

"Eric, why is no one walking in that lane?" she asks pointing to the one all the way on the end.

"Because they're running. Concentrate. You'll see them."

Bailey turns back and concentrates, and Eric is right. It looks like streams of people, some even with their children, racing off like that's just normal to move that fast on a day to day basis. Bailey catches one couple holding hands even!

"So it's like this all the time, three lanes, and we're the slow pokes?"

He smiles, "Yeah, it's like this all the time. We aren't the slow pokes. It isn't a competition. Right now, we're walking slowly because we're in no rush, and also you don't know where we're going, so we don't want to lose you."

"Makes sense. So are you gonna stay here for a..."

"It's right around the corner, Bailey," interrupts Eric's mom. "Here, families live in sections. Is it like that where you live, Bailey?"

"Not where I live. Some places might, but where I live, the rest of our relatives live scattered."

"That's a shame. Safety matters."

Bailey looks over at Eric confused, but Eric just closes his eyes, takes a deep breath and keeps silent for about five seconds before telling her what his mom meant. "I feel like I'm the translator for peace. She doesn't mean it's a shame like a shame. She means that based on how we live here, we need to be ready at all times to help each other, so we live close together, our families do. It's similar to how I helped you when you needed it. You know, I uhh, kinda see you like someone who I'm honored to protect."

"Kinda?" Bailey blushes, thinking about just how much she likes him.

"More than kinda."

"And here we are," interrupts Eric's mom again as they turn the corner into what looks like another world inside this one. "I know it isn't like this where you are from, but we all have different temperatures, and your family tends to be cold when it's hot and hot when it's cold so they keep this big capsule around their residents. Can you see it?"

"No, no, I can't."

"You just don't know what you're looking at. It's clear. You just walked straight through it. Anyway, everyone, let her through."

"Me?" Bailey stops in her tracks as everyone moves to the side. "You want me to knock on the door?"

"Sure, why not? They'll catch on fairly quickly I'm sure."

Eric nods his head, secretly rolling his eyes at his mother's request and accompanies Bailey to the door. Bailey trails slightly behind him, her confidence all out of wack, but she takes a deep breath in order to calm herself as her mind goes all over the place. Suddenly, she loses her train of thought on what she'll say and even what other questions she'll ask after the greeting.

"Eric, wait," she requests as she tugs on his thumb. He stops just before knocking, understanding the question he reads from her desperate eyes.

"It's gonna be fine. Relax. Pretend like you're back on the other side. Imagine... imagine your father," he encourages, "Imagine he's right here with you, and there's a big cookout out back with all the family you've never met, and they can't wait to hug you. They came a long way and have heard so much about you."

"Because we have," says a person swinging open the door. "I've been watching you from inside. You finally came," she says happily. "She's here!" she yells with glee to the others who come immediately from somewhere in the home. About six other people exit and surround Bailey and Eric while Eric's family stands back excitedly watching.

Eric stands there beside Bailey with a big smile on his face, noticing that Bailey isn't budging. There's a smile on her face, but all she's doing is looking around at everyone silently, so he speaks up.

"She's kinda stunned because she had no idea about any of this so she's, I mean, this is new to her, like less than thirty days new and this visit is spur of the moment so she's... and her name is..."

"Shut your mouth, son," his mother whispers, having already crept up behind him. "Let them see her."

Finally, someone older comes from the house. She appears slightly older than what Bailey's father was, and as everyone else backs away, creating aisle for her to approach, Bailey snaps out of her dizzy grin, realizing that this is the actual person that she should be speaking to first.

The woman that approaches Bailey is tall and slender. She wears a long purple cloth that's draped around her like she's the head of some sort of group. She carries herself like she's of most importance, and everyone around her pauses as if she is to be respected. Her hair is braided against her scalp in seven cornrows, the thickest one in the middle. Her hands and feet are the only other parts of her that show beneath the purple drape. All of her fingers are wrapped in laced gold as well as her toes, and her face is undecorated, no make-up or jewelry at all. Flawless she is, and she walks two feet away from Bailey, and finally speaks.

"Welcome home, Bailey. I'm your great aunt. My name is Baileen. Your name comes from me. Your father told me about you a long time ago, and this time has finally come."

"My father told you?" she asks as a lone tear runs down her right cheek. "He didn't hide me?"

"We don't hide our own. There's no reason to do so. Come on and walk with me. You all feel free to go inside. We will be back, and Clivvanna and Johvahn, thank you for bringing her."

"You're welcome, but it was our son, Eric, as you know has been gone forever. He brought her and we just finished the course."

The great aunt Baileen moves over to Eric, places her hand on his, and nods, "Thank you for looking out for her. You will always be welcome. I've heard a little, not much."

"You're welcome, Baileen," Eric responds. "I'm sure she'll fill you in on the rest while we all go inside. Bailey," he calls, "I'll be inside."

She nods and walks off with, whom she now knows is, her beautiful great aunt. Despite being away from Eric in this strange place, she feels so much more at ease because she's actually with family, and not a regular family like back at her home, but with her family that has strange super powers like she does.

As they walk silently, Bailey decides to be the first one to speak. "I didn't know that I was named after you. My dad never told me that I was named after anyone."

"Yes, I know he didn't tell you. I don't think he really would, seeing the circumstances."

"I understand. When did my dad tell you about me?"

"He told me after he left you. He let me know that you were out there, living with your mother, and he asked me to look after you as best that I could. I've tried. Now, I'm glad you're here on this side. I can get a small break," she smiles, noticing the curious expression on Bailey's face. "You want to ask me how I'm looking after you?"

"Yes, please."

"It's one of my gifts. I can't see you, but I can glimpse into your life during the day, but everything looks like shadows. I see you, and only you. I see you..."

"You mean you can see everything I do?"

"Not everything, just glimpses. These glimpses let me know if you're in danger, or if you're fighting, or anything abnormal. Don't worry. It's quite common. Your father can do it as well. He's come and visited you, except he can actually see you."

"That doesn't make me feel too good about my life in the future."

Bailey's aunt looks at her and then unleashes a thunderous laugh. "We can't see anything inappropriate. I can only see whenever you are afraid, bothered, lonely, anything bad. Whenever you're happy, I won't see a thing. That's how I know you're fine. You'll probably see more of your father when you're upset and that's when he will see you most as well. There's normally a need."

"Why? Why does it have to be when there's a need and not a want?"

"Mostly, it's because why waste the view? Would you rather have food when you want it or when you need it if it was limited?"

"I see your point."

"We've been through a lot over here, and we fight wars to keep our people pure. You're an exception."

"Pure?"

"The wars we fought and still fight to keep our belief systems strong because with us, our belief systems alter our physical bodies and more. We all desire to be the best because whenever we do our worst, we lose sight of things. We become more and more like the ones we distrust."

"The Lonthians?"

"Yes, our cousins. There's something about wrong doings. It's a slippery slope, and just like the man your father was after - Xidon – once he went wrong, he remained that way."

"Who says what's wrong here?"

"We know what's wrong when an action produces nothing and destroys all things that produce good. I know of your God. Is that ours as well?"

"You're asking me?"

"Sure."

"Yes, yes. He's the same."

"See. I think I learned that He produces everything for a purpose. Am I right?"

"Yes. And if it has no purpose, then it shouldn't be made, right?"

"I think so."

"And He destroys what doesn't produce good?"

"You're talking about the parable, like the fig tree. My mom used to read me that one all the time. What you say is true, but He also has mercy and forgiveness."

"Yes, and that's what we do, too. His lasts forever, correct?"

"I think so."

"Ours doesn't...our mercy, I mean. We don't know how to do that one yet. In fact, if we leave them alone and let them have their way, they will kill us, too. Is that what mercy means to do?"

"I don't think so. It's okay to defend yourself and your people, but mercy can run out. My mom taught me that God has mercy on us because of our weak state and because he loves us, so I think His mercy is more like parents have for children as we grow up. I understand it that way. We make mistakes, but we do better as we learn better."

"I see. Xidon wasn't like that. Xidon was an assassin and would kill anyone. Your father was after him. He was the only one who gave us a chance. Not many could beat Xidon. You did."

"I had help."

"Your friend."

"Yes."

"You need to build your confidence and your wisdom. You love people and expect the best from them back. This is a mistake. It is a mistake that can make you lose your life if you aren't on guard. It's very hard to kill you, Bailey. Don't make it easy." She pauses her gait and stands, gazing down the path before them before continuing, "Bailey, you must go from here."

"What? Why? What do you mean?" Bailey is stunned at the warning, so much so that she scans the area around her and moves slightly closer to her newfound aunt.

"There's no need to be afraid right now, but you must go and stay away. Not everyone knows that you are a duel, but soon many will know, and your powers aren't that great here. No matter how hard you try, and no matter how much I want you to stay, you cannot. They already know that Xidon has been killed, and if they discover that his killer is here and that you are a duel..."

"They will try and kill me, too."

"They will try, and they will succeed, Bailey. Thankfully, no one knows you're here. No one knows who you are except those of the family, and they all know better than to reveal anything. I ask that you stay for now, and later, don't return. Don't return for your own good. For now," she smiles, "enjoy your family as we will enjoy you. Welcome home."

Bailey smiles as they stroll back to the others, but in the back of her mind, she can't dismiss a sense of dread the closer they get to their destination, like someone's watching her. As they approach the doorway, the sense of dread fades as she finally enjoys the family that she's never known before.

Chapter Four

"And this was him as a little boy."

"Dad never had pictures!" Bailey exclaims as she looks at the images against the glass wall. "He looks the same, just a smaller big head," she laughs along with all her cousins. As she sits in the center of the floor while everyone else gathers around her, she is in awe of the amazing life that it seems Tys have. Everyone is beautiful, with smooth skin and muscular builds. Bailey takes a look at herself, and she clearly understands what her aunt explained to her now. In comparison to them, she appears exceptionally weak! Even Eric looks stronger here.

Quickly sliding down onto the floor beside Bailey, a teenage girl, who happens to resemble her responds, "Yeah, we have plenty pictures of him, but I've never actually met him face to face. There are so many stories. Your dad is like a superhero to us. Do you have fangs, too?" she asks, trying to see through to Bailey's teeth.

"Uh, yeah, uh," she responds hesitantly, looking around for Eric and her aunt. When she sees them, her aunt nods and she continues to answer. "I have fangs just like him." She places her hand over her chest. "Do you...have fangs?"

"No, I don't. My grandfather did though, so I'm not sure how it missed me. If you lived here, you'd probably be one of the first women with fangs."

"What?"

"That's enough," interrupts Bailey's aunt. "I'm sure your new cousin feels a bit out of place. All this is new to her, so don't go making historical references. Pay her no attention, Bailey."

Bailey stands and looks around at how everyone is fawning over her, and then her eyes meet Eric's. Without even saying a word, she knows it's true. "Am I the first girl with fangs, Aunt Baileen?"

"Out!" she roars. "Everyone out!" Immediately, everyone except Eric and his parents leave the room. "You have got to go. You have got to go now, Bailey. I don't have time to explain to you how things work around here, but your cousins aren't as wise as I am."

"Why do I have to leave now? What's going on? Eric?" Bailey asks, but everyone is just as lost as she is. The only one in a panic is her Aunt Baileen, so Eric's mom walks over calmly in an attempt at answers.

"What's going on, Baileen?"

"They heard, and they're coming," she reveals as she moves toward the wall of her home, placing the palms of her hands against it. As she does, her skin begins to vibrate to a rhythm, as if it's transferring a code into her body. Suddenly, she rips her palms away, swiftly charging toward Bailey. "You must leave now!"

Frantically, Eric grabs Bailey's wrist. "Come on, let's go. We have to go!"

"Ericon!" his mother shouts, storming towards him. "I forbid you from staying there with her. I forbid it. You will not leave us this weak. You will not," she orders, lowering her tone to nearly a whisper and slanting her eyes directly at Bailey, before adding. "especially not for her. She's already the cause of my family being weakened as much as it can, and I refuse to let it happen again. I will take her back. Eric, you will remain. That is an order."

Stunned at his mom's harshness, he returns fire, "But you don't even know where to go!" When his mother remains firm on her word, he turns to view Bailey silently weeping and her Aunt Baileen holding her head down in silence as it is customary to never intervene when parents advise or admonish their children. Eric glares in disbelief at his mother, and right before he makes the move to sprint both her and Bailey out, Baileen takes hold of her niece's wrist. "I'll go, Clivvanna. It's my duty to watch after her by the request of her father." Then she looks directly into Clivvanna's eyes. "I'll bring him back. He will not stay, and I won't allow any harm to him or your family on this journey. My word to you goes as far as my life on this side will allow, but we must leave now."

As Baileen speaks, her hair begins to grow at an abnormally rapid rate. The curls in her hair toss and toil with each other until Baileen is draped from her shoulders to her knees, and as she moves to lead us out of the home, Eric's skin grows hotter.

"Eric, what's wrong? What's going on? Is someone coming to kill me?"

"No, just let's go. Let's go now. We're gonna have to walk. I don't know where we're gonna land but... Mom and dad, leave. Leave now. You can't fight."

"We must," his father boldly replies, ignoring his weakness and the shame it will bring to him and his family if he doesn't protect them with his life, but Eric's mother chimes in immediately.

"None of us have to fight. Who they want is right here. We can just hand her over. It's her fight. It's always been her fight. The fight of the fathers lands on the children. It's the way it's always been, and who are we to intervene? We know how this will end up, Baileen, no matter what."

"Mom, enough!" Eric's voice shakes the entire home, causing the beautiful, bright purple and green vines to fall from the invisible ceiling, landing all around their feet. Bailey tries to escape his hand out of fear, but he secures it in his. "Don't be afraid. You never have to fear me." He turns to her. "You know this. This is who I am here. Mom, we're leaving from right here."

Before his mother interjects, Bailey sees several bodies surrounding the home, and all her cousins come from the back, each one angry in appearance and seemingly ready to display their anger in a brawl.

"Go now! Eric, do you know the code?" Baileen shouts as her hair conceals Eric and Bailey. "Eric, do you know the code to return her back?"

"Yes, I'm trying. Give me a second," he stresses, trying to concentrate on something behind his eyes.

"Unlock it! Do it now!"

Eric's eyes move rapidly behind his eyelids, like he's in the middle of a nightmare, when they finally stop. "Mom, I'll come back. I will. Now listen to me Bailey. Look into my eyes. We're all alone. Become one with me, and don't be afraid. You can see them but they can't see you. We have to go. Don't turn your eyes to look. Just look at me or we won't make it."

Bailey continues to tremble, finding it most difficult to terminate the shudders and even harder to not pay attention to the bodies of s that pile against her aunt's home. Eric continues speaking to her, but she can't focus until finally he says something that grabs her complete attention.

"I love you, Bailey. Come with me."

Chapter Five

"They wanna kill me!"

"Wait. I don't know where we are. Do you?"

"Since they know how the trick to open up the portal thing like you do, are they coming behind us?"

"No. They have to stand in the same spot to get to where we are right now, and more than likely, a fight is about to brew so I have to get you back home so I can go back."

"Go back! Go back to fight?"

"Yes, oh... I see where we are. Come on. Hop on my back."

"Why?"

"Because I run faster than you."

"But, Eric..."

"Bailey!" he finally shouts. "My dad is in there with your aunt. I have a family, too, and did you see those s? I have to go back." He quiets down. "I'm gonna try to get back right here because the path has already been made, but if not, I'm leaving again from your backyard because that path is set directly to my house in Tylon. I can run there when I get there. Come on." He watches as the tears swell in her eyes. "I'll be back. Trust me."

She hops on his back and in five seconds, she's back at her home, and he leaves without a good-bye. When she goes to the backyard to see if he is still there, he isn't. He's really gone back to Tylon.

Climbing back through her window, she undresses, puts on her pajamas and heads down the hallway to peep in on her sleeping mother. She hasn't even moved from her position since Bailey fled on her trip to another dimension. So much has occurred within those couple of hours that it's difficult for Bailey to gather all of it together and make sense of it.

Slowly sliding beneath her warm covers, she stacks her pillows to sit up as she grabs her journal which sits in the drawer of the nightstand beside her bed. She then turns on the lamp and starts writing all she remembered, from the time she was taken from her yard into another dimension which seemed to be right next door. There wasn't a tunnel like in the movies and there wasn't a harsh wind or terrible tumble into the destination. In the blink of an eye, they were in Tylon and just like that, she's back home in her bed.

As she scribbles as fast as she can, using as much detail as she can remember so that the words paint a complete picture of Tylon and the people, she soon starts to wonder when one of the Lonthians will cross over to find her and possibly kill her in revenge of not only Delight but Delight's father, Xidon.

"There were three walkways, like highway sidewalks or something. There were no cars anywhere but everyone sped in the farthest side and there's a slow side where regular walking beings walked. In the middle there the average speed walkers," she states as her pen starts to die. Shaking it and trying again, she scribbles a bunch of lines on the paper, and as she does, the sound of something shuffling outside her bedroom window startles her. Quickly, she wonders if it's Eric, but she's too afraid to look out her window. Therefore, she sends him a text message and waits, but nothing happens. Afraid that someone from Tylon is outside trying to kill her, she slides down onto the floor and silently slides beneath the window. That's when she hears another sound, causing her to throw both her hands over her mouth to keep from screaming.

She places her hands over her heart and takes deep breaths, convincing herself to calm down, completely afraid of all the noise outside of her window. Could it be them, the Lonthians? Could this be the day that she has to fight for her life? Why did she even go to Tylon? All the hypotheticals that chase her out of her comfort reach at tipping point until she finally decides to pull back her curtains and look outside.

As she meets her fears head on, she takes a deep breath realizing that there's nothing there but one of the branches from the tree that shades a portion of her house, broken and leaning over at her window. She unlocks and slides the window up, reaches for the rather thick broken limb and yanks. It doesn't fall right away, so she yanks on it a couple more times, and it still doesn't budge enough to break apart from the tree. When she lets it go, it bangs into her window once again, but then she stops.

A chill runs up and down her spine and chill bumps cover her arms as she remembers when Eric dropped her back at home at this same window. The tree limb wasn't broken. Quickly, she glances up in to the tree, but it's too dark to see much, and then she peers out into the night. Everything is still. Stillness doesn't break tree limbs.

Frightened, she slams the window back down and locks it, double checking by trying to shove it up with all her strength. When it doesn't move, she closes her curtains and backs away from the window slowly until she bumps into a figure, causing her so much horror that she erupts into a terrified scream.

"Bailey!"

"Mom!" she shouts as she turns around, grabbing her mom in desperation. Confused her mom looks back at the window and then back at Bailey.

"Why did you just slam the window? Why did you even have it open so late? What's going on? Is someone out there?" she asks, shoving Bailey behind her and going toward the window to look out. "And if there is someone out there, why on earth would you open the window, Bailey? And what happened to the tree?" she asks as the limp comes forward and knocks the window again. "It's gonna break the window eventually, that's for sure."

"It scared me, so that's what happened. It caught me off guard and I wasn't thinking so I opened it up and tried to fix it, and I don't know. I got scared."

"Don't be. It's just a limb, but how on earth..."

"That's the thing. I don't know. It's like something must have been standing on it. Something big had to have been standing on it."

"What? Like a bear?"

"I don't know."

"We didn't have any storm either."

"That's why I got scared. Limbs just don't do that."

"And not limbs on this healthy tree anyway. Listen, tomorrow, I will buy one of those small saws and we can saw it off. Sound good? Now go back to sleep. If you want to, we can switch rooms or you can just come in here with me. Here, I have an idea. Help me push your dresser in front of this window, just in case it breaks. That way, the window will still be blocked."

They both shove the heavy dresser in front of the window, and as Bailey's mom backs away from it to make sure it's doing what she wants it to do, she makes a final decision. "Yeah, you sleep in my room, and I'm going to sleep in here. I sleep lighter than you do, and ..."

"No!" Bailey shouts, scared of what her mother doesn't know and should never know, at least not now. "I mean, I'm not that heavy a sleeper. You go ahead and go into your bedroom, and I'll be okay. You think I wouldn't hear not only the window crack but a whole dresser move if someone was coming in? The dresser in front of the window was genius."

"You alright, Bailey?" her mom asks, looking her over and then turning all around to locate something that will clue her in as to why Bailey is so jumpy.

"Yeah, Ma. I'm fine. I just got shook up a little by the noise, so you know how adrenaline is when you get scared, and now, I have to wait on it to go back down. I probably won't even go back to sleep, no matter where I lay my head, for a good hour. Anyway, mom, trust me, now that you checked on everything and I checked before you, everything is fine."

Instead of standing there listening, Bailey's mother walks back to her bedroom and seconds later, exits her bedroom with pillows in arms, enters Bailey's bedroom once again just to plant herself on the other side of the bed. "Goodnight, Bailey. Stand there, get in the bed or go in my bedroom, but there's no way I will get any sleep knowing that a whole branch may knock your window out in the middle of the night."

For a minute, Bailey just stands there until finally, giving up, placing her hand over here chest to cover the fang on her chest, climbs inside the bed and lies next to her mother, who ten minutes later, is already asleep. With her back to her mom, she stares into the darkness until the wall focuses in and about ten minutes later, she slides from the bed, grabs her journal and walks into the dining room to finish writing all she can remember about Tylon.

Chapter Six

"What are you doing here? I haven't heard from you since Tylon, and now you just pop up after not texting me or anything?" she asks on the first day back to school since everything went down. Eric is situated across the hall behind her, and with her newfound powers, she is able to sense him really well without even turning around. Her senses have been up since she left Tylon. It's fear she supposes, and she can sense everything with so much more accuracy than she ever has before.

"I had to come back, but I'm not here to stay for long. I had to take care of something that I didn't want to take care of like this, but I had no choice," he says from the other side of the hallway. His tone is low, at a whisper. He's barely opening his mouth as he speaks, but Bailey hears every word. "I had to tell my folks down here who I really am, Bailey. They act like they don't know me anymore. They don't understand," he says as his voice cracks, causing Bailey to spin around because she can feel the hurt in his voice.

"Eric," she calls, turning around to face him. His eyes are full of tears, but before she let them fall in front of everyone, she walks over, takes him by the hand and they go to the back of the school. It's lunchtime, but she plans on skipping today.

"So, I didn't think you were ever coming back, and when you didn't text me or anything..."

"I didn't want to text you when I got back, and for the record, Bailey, I can't text you from Tylon."

"Oh...I didn't know. That's obvious though, huh?"

"Should be. Pretty much."

"Yeah, sorry."

"Anyway, when I got back, my folks here hadn't seen me, so they were worried, so in order to make them feel better, I told them who I really am."

"So they believed you?"

"That's the thing. They didn't believe me at first, so I had to show them. I didn't want to but I had to so they wouldn't be afraid for me. When I showed them my speed, they both had to sit down."

"They sat?"

"Yeah, for a long time. Neither one of them went to work. They were in a daze, and as they sat down, I cleaned the house and cooked them a nice dinner."

"You did all that?"

"Yeah, and then like thirty minutes later, they finally said something."

"It's gonna be okay."

"It's gonna be okay?"

"Yeah. That's what they said. I asked them not to tell anyone because it's fairly dangerous to me if they do so, and they agreed. Now though, they're acting really weird. It's like they are walking around like undercover operatives. It's strange," he laughs.

"You mean they aren't angry and you aren't sad?"

"What made you think that?" he sarcastically laughs.

"You faked it to get me over here next to you," she sighed, rolling her eyes, about to go back to where she was but he softly touches the tips of her fingers, and the touch holds her there.

"I faked some of it. I faked the reason for the tears in my eyes, but the tears were real. Bailey, I have to stay in Tylon right now, and I've never felt a pain like this. I stopped by school to tell you. My folks say they will withdraw me so it will be a clean leave. I told them about how I feel about you, too."

Bailey remains silent because she doesn't know what to say. She hasn't even come to grips with her true emotions for Eric, and now that he's leaving, her emotions are in even worse turmoil. She stands there recalling vividly how sternly his mother relayed those same words to her about Eric having to stay. The threat was real. The energy she felt coming from Clivvanna was one of the most powerful threats she'd ever felt, and she warned her without raising her voice or her finger.

Finally, Bailey stares through her tears and tells him without more than a second of hesitation, "Then go." And although she feels glued to him via their touch, she rips her fingertips from his, turns and makes her way to class, her head high though the tears seem to cause deep gulfs down her cheeks.

No one questions her tears when she enters the classroom. No one dares. They figure they know why she's crying, and they're right. She's loosing everyone she loves. Everyone.

As she slumps down in her seat, the teacher continues teaching, her peers continue scribbling notes and she sits there watching them all. Everyone's life seems the same, except for her own. Everything is easy – the way they all smile and really mean it as well as the way they all appear interested in the science lesson that's going on. Everyone is paying attention, but no one is really paying any attention at all. They have no idea that Bailey is not the same anymore, and that she'll never be.

When class is over, Bailey remains seated until everyone leaves the room and it's just herself and the teacher there. As the teacher prepares for the next class, she's stunned when she turns around and finds Bailey still seated.

"Bailey?" The teacher doesn't realize it, but Bailey is listening intently to all the conversations in the hallway. She's waiting until the people begin to disperse before she wants to go out. "Bailey, I know you've had to be strong during such a rough year for you. If you need to go home, I will most certainly write you a pass."

Immediately, Bailey stops listening to the voices beyond the walls so that she can focus in on the teacher's heart beat. Then, she finally responds, "Yes, please."

"Sure thing, dear." She walks back towards her desk. "Now you go straight to the office so they can dismiss you. I know how you feel believe it or not. I lost my mother when I was only thirteen years old, a bit younger than you. That pain, some people say it gets easier to bear. Not me. I say that pain, you just grow to be strong enough to hold it so it doesn't weigh you down. Sometimes, in order to understand something," she says walking back toward Bailey's desk with the pass, "you have to examine it from the other side. Here you are."

She holds out the pass, but before Bailey takes it, she stands from her desk and says, "Thank you." Then she leaves class without the pass.

Chapter Seven

"Eric!" she calls as she runs toward the class he's supposed to be in, but he isn't there. To her, this means he's out of school and either at his house or officially gone back to Tylon. Her heart sinks, and she runs out of the school on the way to his house in hopes that he returned. By the time she gets there, she 's winded, but she doesn't try and gain her composure. Instead, she knocks and rings the doorbell. Not much time goes by before someone swings the door open.

The woman that stands there before Bailey has bloodshot eyes and walking up behind her is a man who reaches out, placing his hands gently on her shoulder. He speaks.

"Come on in, Bailey." His voice is deep and stern, and it's evident that he's going through something terrible. Bailey, without even speaking, breaks down in tears at the door, and at that point, Eric's adoptive parents usher her inside and shut the door behind her.

"I'm sorry. I asked Eric to take me to Tylon, and if I'd never asked him to take me, he would still be here," Bailey cries. "I'll try and get him to come back, I promise I will." She wipes her eyes and looks up, and Eric's adoptive parents have backed away from her in shock.

"You mean to tell me you too?"

"What do you mean? I thought he told you..."

"No, we knew about you. Sure, he told us about you and even showed us your picture in his phone, but you're from this place called Tylon as well? We had no idea!"

"No, no ma'am, I'm not from Tylon. My father was. He's gone now. He passed away in a crash, so I'm half Ty. Just half. Eric – he's full. I just found out myself, but don't tell anyone because my mom she..." Bailey trails off.

"Child, your own mother doesn't know?"

"No, ma'am, she doesn't, so please keep this a secret just like you're keeping Eric's heritage a secret," Bailey asks, "Please."

"We won't discuss this with anyone, Bailey. Come on and sit down," Eric's stepfather promises.

"Call me Mike and this is my wife, Andrea. We uhhh...we had to let Eric go back to that place called Tylon because he said his real parents needed him, something about his father's strength was weak, but that's all we know. Let me ask you something. Is it possible that we can all go up there – or wherever it is – to see the place, to see him?" he asks curiously, holding his wife's hand because she's clearly distraught by the whole situation. "My wife and I really connected with Eric as our son, and we love him, and the thought that he might need us for anything at all..."

"Mr. Mike, trust me, he knows exactly where to find you, and I can assure you that he loves you, too, or he would never have come back to tell you. As far as you going to Tylon, I don't know how to take you. I don't even know how to get there, not without Eric. All I know is there are these portals, but how to connect with them, I don't know. I've never even seen them. It's like a teleport of some sort, and I don't know how to do it." Bailey stands up and prepares to leave, afraid that she may say too much about herself and Eric unintentionally. "I need

to leave now. I just needed to catch him because…"
she drifts off into her mind, not allowing the words *I
love him* to be stated. She then proceeds to exit the
home, leaving his stepparents calling for her to wait.
She doesn't listen. Instead, she runs.

Bailey runs all the way home. She doesn't
stop. She's not running fast nor is she running at a
slow pace, but there's an energy there that keeps her
going nonstop until she reaches her home. When
she arrives, she isn't even out of breath. She
assumes it's because of her inheritance from her
father, something that she has yet to figure out, but
she isn't trying to figure it out at all at the moment.
All she wants to do is see Eric again, so she takes all
the time she needs to release her emotions in tears
before her mother comes home from work, finding it
difficult to believe that all of this is not her fault.

"Don't cry, Bailey," says a familiar voice out
of nowhere.

Bailey's head jolts up and her tears dry up
just as fast as they came tumbling out. The voice is
very familiar. It sounds like the voice of someone
that she's met recently – Baileen, her aunt from

Tylon. The voice comes again, but this time much fainter, so she stands to listen.

"Eric is here with us, and I need to tell you that danger is near you. There is a war brewing, Bailey. Keep your mother close. They will come after..."

The voice stops, and Bailey panics. "Hello? Hello, Aunt Baileen? Hello! What about my mom? What war?! How do they even know my mom?"

At this point, Bailey is terrible shaken, and she finds no possible way to focus on one thought because all of the thoughts she has lead only to her mother. As her stomach quakes, she speeds to the bathroom to vomit. Grabbing the side of the bathtub as she stabilizes herself, she rubs her chest as her heart throbs and the fang on her chest begins to deliver so much pain that she crouches over once again until suddenly, she tastes blood.

As she rubs her tongue across her teeth, all the memories of the day she had to take the life of her friend come storming back, and she realizes that she's in immediate danger. If she wasn't, her fangs wouldn't be pushing their way out. As she covers her mouth, she stares back at the bathroom entrance, knowing that someone must be there to harm her. Fear overpowers her, and she can't move just thinking about the warning sent to her just minutes ago from her aunt in Tylon.

Pushing herself from the sides of the bathtub, she feels the gush of blood rush into her mouth as the fangs emerge. Her chest begins to ache, centered at the first fang that she lost in her battle with Delight. *"Don't let anyone kill you"* are the words she recalls her Ty aunt tell her, and as soon as she senses the presence directly behind her, she lashes out, throwing all the power and might of her fists behind her, but they don't hit anything. Instead, they destroy the wall tiles which come crashing to the floor.

The danger is still present, but unseen. She can feel it, and once she feels the presence again, she lunges toward the invisible and doesn't hit a thing before she is knocked to the floor and then dragged down the hallway from out of the bathroom. Bailey doesn't kick and scream as she is yanked viciously by her shirt, but instead, she creates skid marks all the way down the hallway, and even lifts some of the hardwood floor up from its position as she slams her feet into it, trying to create a full stop. When that doesn't work, she lifts her body as if she's a professional gymnast off the floor, flipping herself up to the ceiling to create more space between herself and the unseen attacker and then with all the power she can muster, she kicks herself down toward the only thing she can see – the floor – in hopes to grab whatever or whoever is after her. With her hands sealed shut and swinging with all the force inside her, hoping to destroy everything attacking her on the way down, she careens into the floor, leaving a deep hole in the living room floor. Then, suddenly, out of nowhere, everything is still and her fangs start to recede as there's a knock on the front door.

Startled and spinning to face the door with her fists still in the air, she quietly tip toes over to it and looks through the peephole. It's Eric. She immediately opens the door, shaken so much that she can't speak.

Chapter Eight

"I know," Eric consoles her. "I know. I got here as soon as I could," he continues as Bailey releases all of her tension of tears and fears onto his chest. His heart is racing as if he'd been fighting.

"Were you here? Did you rescue me again?"

"No, no, not this time. By the looks of it though, you weren't an easy win."

She looks back at the destruction to her home, and immediately sulks. "No, don't let that fool you. I was a very easy win. I'm not sure what happened. My fangs were out and whatever it was, I couldn't..."

"Too fast?"

"Yeah, too fast, and I guess when whatever it was dragged me out of the bathroom..."

"Wait. You didn't see who it was while you were being dragged either?"

"No, no," she responds confused. "Why?"

Eric walks further inside the house and gives it further inspection. "Where did he drag you from?

From where? Here?" he asks, looking down at the floor at the place where Bailey first dug her heels into the hardwoods.

"Yeah, right there," she says, wiping her mouth. "There's still blood on my…"

"No. Don't wipe it. Go to the sink and make sure it goes down the drain. Throw me a rag out of the bathroom. Hurry," he advises as Eric stands on guard flipping the rooms inside and out with his powers to see behind the walls. When Bailey returns, he quickly starts to wipe any spot of blood from the destroyed floors, walls and furniture as Bailey runs back into the bathroom to do as instructed – rinse her blood down the sink.

Eric enters the bathroom, handing her the towel. "You must remember that if any enemy touches your blood, they can harm you. Your blood…"

"Is an extension of my body." She drops her eyes in heartfelt pain. "Delight told me that as she attacked me. Why didn't I feel you as you touched my blood?"

"First, I didn't touch it. I used a towel. Secondly," he states as he reaches for her face, "I'm not your natural born enemy. You missed some." He wipes her cheek and shows her the blood on his thumb. "Your body is made to detect enemies. Why would you need to detect true friends and people who love you and wish you no harm? This is your special sense."

"You love me," she states, not in disbelief but convincing herself that is what he said.

"Yeah. I almost gave my life for you, didn't I? I love you, Bailey. We have known each other for..."

"A long time. I love you, too."

The front door slams. "Bailey! Bailey! Oh my Lord, Bailey, baby!" her mother enters, taken aback by the state of the room and how the floor is beat up. Bailey rushes from the bathroom, while Eric remains inside, hesitant to make his first meeting with Bailey's mother under such extreme circumstances. He wants to disappear, but before he gets the nerve to speed run, Bailey's mother appears at the bathroom door having followed the broken hardwoods right to him.

Eric takes a deep breath, swallows and introduces himself as she stands glaring at him. "I'm Eric, Mrs..."

"Call me Lynette, and why are you in the bathroom with my child, and why does my house look like a brawl?" Then she looks into the sink, then back at her daughter. "What's going on?"

Thirty Minutes Later

"It's inside your chest?"

Bailey takes her mother's hand and rubs it across the outline of the fang inside her chest. Her mother then passes out on the couch – again. Eric picks up the towel filled with ice, hands it to Bailey and she places it across her mother's chest.

"I don't think you should've let her feel it."

"Well, she sort of asked, Eric. What was I supposed to do?"

Suddenly, Lynette's eyes open, and she shuffles herself back up. "You were attacked in here by someone from a different dimension in a place called..."

"Yes, from Tylon," Eric states, "and Bailey is half Ty because..."

"...of Dad. It was Dad, Mom. Dad," she stutters, "And now that he's gone, I inherited all his powers sorta and more than what I think I even want."

"How long have you had that fang in your chest, Bailey?" she asks, reaching out to voluntarily touch it this time. Bailey glances over at Eric, and Eric shakes his head. Therefore, she keeps it a secret. She can never tell her mother what happened to Delight, not ever.

"Well, it just happened to grow there, right after dad died. It grew in slowly, so ... and I didn't want to make a fuss over it, especially after Eric let me know, and Dad let me know..."

"Wait what?"

Eric puts his hand on Bailey's shoulder, hoping that she will keep more to herself.

"Dad, uhh, he uhh..." Bailey stalls, unable to think up something other than the truth. "He told me, after he died. He told me. He visited me. He said it would be fine, and that all is well. It happens."

"Bailey, your father is dead."

"Mrs. Lynette, uhh, Lynette, what she means is that Tys don't die all the way. We can return sporadically to see our loved ones, and even speak, just not touch."

"You mean, when I saw him the other night it wasn't my imagination?"

"It probably wasn't, Ma."

Bailey's mom stands and walks over to the floor. "Why are they attacking you again, and why should I protect myself?"

"Because Dad was a soldier where he's from, not just a truck driver, and after he'd captured a known assassin, apparently, they wanted to get him but he passed away before they could and now they're after me. But don't worry, Ma, because I have these fangs that keep me..."

"Okay! I have to go back home now," Eric interrupts, widening his eyes as he walks directly in front of Bailey. "I will keep my eyes on you two. I have to go now." He turns back to Bailey's mom. "I'm sorry we had to meet on such not-so-ordinary terms, but hopefully, you know how much I respect you and Bailey."

"Thank you," Lynette reaches out to touch his hand. "Thank you for coming when you did, and ... and ... I don't know what else to say."

"I can feel it," he says, softly squeezing her hand. "See you later." In seconds, Eric is gone. Seconds later, Lynette grabs Bailey and hugs her tighter than what she's ever hugged her in her life.

"I'm not going to let anything happen to you. Not ever."

Bailey doesn't answer. Instead she weeps at the fact that her mom has no control of any of what's going on. Everything is on her shoulders. She has to make sure nothing happens to her mother. It's either that or break her mother's heart but turning herself over to the Lonthians.

Chapter Nine

Bailey sleeps in her mother's bedroom at bedtime, and for most of the night, she is wide awake. Her mother had locked the doors and double checked all the windows, as well as placing alarms on each one. Bailey watched her mother consume herself with worry and anxiety over all she'd learned during the second half of the day.

They both tried to patch of the broken pieces of hardwood floor so they wouldn't catch a splinter inside their feet. It didn't work so they ended up scooting the sofa over the worst parts of the floor until hiring a repairman. The whole time they were fixing the living room back to normal as much as possible, Lynette inspected Bailey nonstop. She didn't know what to do, say, or if she should even believe it. At one point she was looking for hidden cameras, assuming that she was being set up to look crazy on a television show before the nation. It wasn't until Bailey stopped in the middle of the floor and then disappeared before her mother's eyes that her mother knew everything was real. Lynette hasn't been the same since.

"Mom, I'm not asleep, and I know you aren't really asleep either. You don't have to be afraid. You can't protect me, but I can protect you. I will protect you." Her mom doesn't respond. "Mom?"

"I hear you, Bailey. You went to that place you say your father is from?" she asks as more tears flow from her eyes. "I never knew. Why didn't he ever…"

"Mom, he never could have taken you. It doesn't work like that. I'm duel heritage. You aren't. They can come here, but we can't go there – regular people."

"To which you aren't anymore," she responds, turning over onto her back to stare at the ceiling before reaching over to squeeze Bailey's hand. "I love you so much, and I wouldn't have ever tried to put you in this position if I would have known. He should've told me. He should've told me something!" she cries, her emotions breaking through, causing her to release them all through banging her fist against the bed.

"Mom, don't be angry that he fell in love with you. If he didn't, I wouldn't be here. I don't know why he never told you, but maybe he will tell you himself one day why he didn't."

She laughs hysterically, but the laugh is pure pain, so Bailey turns to face her. "Mom, Dad really can come back. You really did see him. It isn't a lie. I think he comes back to see you, and sometimes when you think it's your imagination, it really isn't. The next time he visits me, I will ask him to ..."

"You shouldn't have to ask him, Bailey. It's something he should do if he knows he can," she responds sternly. "It's not enough that he left, but he won't comfort me by letting me know he's okay? Why?"

"Mom, I don't know, but trust me, he has his reasons. I don't know the reason, but I know he has one. If you only knew... and I met my aunt in Tylon."

"Your aunt?"

"My great aunt. Dad had already told her about me, and she can see me sometimes, see through dimensions, but she can only see my shadow. They knew about Dad being married. He didn't keep you a secret, Ma. He didn't keep us a secret, but it's good now that most things are secret. It's for the best. Mom, they really want to kill me, and I shoudn't have ever gone to Tylon because they've seen me. I can't hide. I have to fight, and I can. I really can. I'm the best," she explains, trying to convince and make her mother feel better because she doesn't even believe it. "You can sleep. My fangs warn me if we are in danger."

"Bailey, I'm so sorry," she cries as they embrace.

"It's okay, Mom. We're fine. We have a whole bunch of people watching after us, too, including Dad."

The Next Day Afterschool

Instead of taking the bus back home, Bailey decides to do something she hasn't done since she had to fight and destroy Delight in the alley. She hasn't gone to see her Delight's mother. She stayed from anywhere near the scene of the battle that ended the life of her best friend, but now that time has gone by, she feels that she needs to check on Delight's mom since, from what she recalls, there is no one else besides her mother left.

As she passes by the alley where she involuntarily killed Delight, she keeps her attention on the sidewalk, playing a childhood game of "Don't Step on the Crack". Cautiously, she rolls her tongue over her teeth, making certain she doesn't feel anything warning her of an impending attack. The small hairs on arm stand at attention as she moves by the battle location, and as soon as she is a good distance away from it, she calms down.

She can see Delight everywhere in her imagination. They used to hang-out just about everywhere over here. Life is so different now that she's gone, and strangely enough, she hasn't been visited by her at all. Bailey even wonders if she can being that she's a duel like she is.

Finally, she arrives at Delight's home, and she takes a deep breath before knocking on the door. Her throat quakes, and she shivers before the front door opens. There Delight's mother stands with tears in her bloodshot eyes. She's been crying. Without hesitation, Bailey embraces her, and they both begin weeping uncontrollably as Bailey repeatedly apologizes. After the tearful greeting, they both go sit inside her sewing room as she finishes alterations.

"Have a seat in that chair right there, Bailey, and thank you for stopping by. I was wondering when you were gonna come check on an old, lonely lady. Now that everything is over, people have to get back to their normal lives, and I can't get angry when they forget about my broken heart and soul."

Bailey wipes her eyes and tries to un-see what she did. She even starts to question why she's even visiting with Delight's mother as she is the killer. Bailey starts feeling nauseated and starts to get up, but Delight's mother stops her verbally as she watches from her periphery.

"Don't flee. You're okay. You know, if I were in your position, I would take deep breaths, just close my eyes and take some deep breaths." She presses the foot pedal and the sewing machine needle enters in out of the cloth as her fingertips guide the cloth. "Go on, Bailey. Take deep breaths. I need your company here, so don't leave just yet. Close your eyes and take slow deep breaths. I used to want to study therapy, you know? That's another love of mine. I'm using it to get through this as best I can. Go ahead and try it."

Bailey slides back into the chair, leans her head onto the wall and then does what she's told – close her eyes and deep breathe. Behind her eyelids, she sees Delight. Tears roll down her face as she continues to follow Delight's jovialness through the halls of school and her sharp wit when she claps back at someone whenever necessary. Just imagining her still here, brings a little bit of joy, so much so that she wipes the tears and smiles a bit before opening her eyes to Delight's mother's face two inches from hers.

"I know why you're here!" she scolds, causing Bailey to leap from the chair. Scared, she covers her mouth, but there's no need because her fangs aren't protruding from her gums despite her bring startled. "I know exactly why you're here, Bailey. You're her kind. I knew she was who she was before she even knew. Her father told me. Do you hear me? Her father told me, and I regretted ever meeting him."

She turns her back to Bailey and walks to the opposite wall. "Delight only knew good things about her dear old dad, but I knew he was *nothing*. I couldn't leave him, so I was happy he was dead. What I didn't know was that *your father* was the one that killed him," she states before laughing with tears rolling down her face. "Oh boy, how I would hate *pretending* to be sad for his death in front of Delight. I wanted her to shout for joy, but I didn't want her to become like him ever. I felt like if I could just raise her like me." Then, she turns to face Bailey. "Raise her like a real human instead of half human, half monster. Her dad was a monster, and it was impossible for me to get away from him. The only reason, and I mean the only reason, he was with me was to have a seed here. Somehow, he knew his time was coming short because he'd seen his rival."

Delight's mother eyes Bailey like she's trying to figure something out. Bailey refuses to confirm her story or deny it as tears roll down her face. "I just came to see how you were doing is all. I don't know..."

"Did you take my daughter from me, Bailey? Don't lie, Bailey. I know you and her have the same powers. I would sneak and watch her, you know, before she was killed. She changed. I tried my best to make her forget about her father, but the more time went on, the more she had an anger that grew just like her father's. It was like I saw him inside her, his literal being, and he was thirsty for blood. Then, I noticed how you all hadn't been speaking and how she began wishing..."she pauses, "you were dead and how she was going to kill you. So, Bailey, don't be afraid. I figured it all out. Did you take my daughter from me, Bailey?"

"I have to go, Mrs. Bernice." Bailey flees from the house, not looking back because she knows Delight's mother is right behind her and she feels the blood drip onto her tongue. Bursting through the door, she speeds all the way home, and as she locks the door, she leans over to pull the sofa over in front of it. The sofa feels as light as a feather. Then, she rushes into the bathroom and vomits, in disbelief that Delight's mom was about to try and kill her. There was no doubt, because she's spitting blood from her mouth.

Chapter Ten

"Are you okay?"

"Yeah, yeah, I'm fine. Come around to the front and I'll let you in," Bailey tells Eric who popped up unannounced. When she opens the front door, Eric rushes inside.

"Your aunt told me to get here fast, that you were in danger, but now you aren't. I just had to..."

"Well, I'm fine," Bailey says, holding in her sorrow as she walks away from Eric who stands there reading her like a book that he's read one thousand times.

"You're not fine. Who tried to hurt you? Your aunt said it was a woman, a real human? Where were you?"

"I went to Delight's house."

"You did what? Why?"

"Because I had to! I wanted to check on her mother, Eric. That was my best friend's mom, and I killed her daughter! That's why and I feel like the worst person in the world because I have no one to talk to and you left me here to deal with it all and figure it all out, and I didn't know she knew!"

"She knows?" he asks alarmed. "How does she know you killed..."

Bailey throws her hands in the air. "No, no...she doesn't know that for sure," she says, lowering her voice, "but she has a sure hunch because she put the pieces of the puzzle together based on Delight's behavior prior to her death. She even knew about Delight's father being from Tylon. I didn't see her try and attack me. I ran because I felt my fangs and I tasted blood on the way out. I knew she couldn't catch me, and I didn't want to kill her."

"Come here, Bailey. I'm sorry. It's not like I don't care, but I'm from Tylon, and I see things from a different angle than you." He hugs her and explains again that his only concern is her safety. "I'm Ty. There's always a point where my emotions will cut off for survival and logic."

Bailey pulls back, not fully understanding what he means. "Are you saying that you can stop caring about someone just like that?"

"No. What I am saying is that my heart doesn't always guide me. I don't have to always feel it, so I don't have to always use it, not like you where it seems that beings on this side have that side of them on at all times. We from Tylon have to allow it. Did you not see how I have known Delight, too, but I didn't shed a tear in the alley?" Bailey backs away from him, slightly afraid of what he's saying, but he continues. "Once something has to be done, Bailey, it must be done. Her father would have never stopped killing through her, even after he'd have killed you. He was an assassin. He is."

"What if it was my dad who was the assassin, Eric?"

"It wasn't."

"But what if it was? What if I was in Delight's position?"

"I could have never been drawn to you, not like this. We would never have been in this situation that we are in now. It's an impossibility, Bailey."

"Will you ever turn on me?"

"Bailey..."

"Will you?"

"No," he pauses, "No. I died for you, remember? That's why my dad is in the condition he is now."

"I just needed to know."

"You just don't turn on me, okay?"

"Yeah, okay, but now what do I do? Delight's mom is onto me. What if she goes to the police?"

"Did you tell her you did it?"

"No."

"Well, you didn't. Anyway, we need to give your Ty side a name because you aren't Bailey when you're her. What name do you think would work for the Ty you?"

"I don't know. I never thought about it."

"Well let's come on over here and sit down on this couch that I see you moved and figure it out before I go back. I have a couple minutes," he says smiling, taking her hand and walking with her over to the sofa. "I want you to feel better before I go. You're in no real danger at this minute, so relax and let's figure out who you are now."

"I'm Bailey."

"No, you're," he sings as they both sit. "Go ahead, I'm waiting."

"I don't know. Speedy?"

"Speedy?" he laughs. "No. You hardly run faster than me. You're not fast like that in comparison to the fastest in Tylon, so you can't be Speedy. Plus, it's corny. Sounds horrible. You don't know what you look like do you, when you change."

"No, I've never seen myself."

"You look like yourself, but more cut, stronger and your skin is bold, between a smooth black and a dark brown metallic. Don't think of it as a cartoon or anything, but that's the only way I can describe it on this side."

"Sort of like how you look in Tylon? I saw you, you looked different. I knew it was you, but you looked different, good and different."

"Well, you do as well. You're beautiful, now and when you change. No one on this side will recognize you though because your Ty skin isn't like any skin on this side. The only person who could possibly recognize you is your mom, Black Fang." He leans back with his eyes squinted and his arms and legs shielding his body like he was preparing for an all out attack.

"Black Fang?" Bailey asks before reaching up to rub the permanent fang in her chest.

"You like? I didn't want you to have of our odd names, and plus I like to watch your superhero movies, so I thought it should be more of your lingo. Black Fang defines you, in both ways."

Bailey doesn't immediately respond. Instead, she sits with it, rehearsing the name in her head before finally giving Eric a smile. "I like it." Then, she stands up, walks around the living room area and repeats, "I like it, but what do I do with it?"

"What do you mean?" Eric responds curiously.

"Like am I supposed to ..."

Quickly predicting what she's about to say, "No. That's just your name is all. No movie stuff. Trust me, you, me or any of us won't end up like in the movies – celebrated and venerated. Instead we will end up chased, mutilated and caged."

"You think?" she jokes.

"It's no joking matter. You know that. Just keep it in house. The next time you ever visit Tylon, you can be looser. Until then, just be regular Bailey unless you're in danger." He goes over to her. "I love you, Black Fang."

"I love you, too. Come back to see me, okay? Not just when I'm in danger."

"Yeah, okay." They embrace, and then he walks out the door, reminding her to be confident, not careless, strong and not arrogant."

As she watches him walk to the back of the house through the window, she says to herself, "I'll try... but I don't know how that's gonna turn out." She giggles as she leaps around the house calling herself Black Fang. "Madame Black Fang. Black Fangstress!" she sings as she starts cleaning the house, forgetting all her troubles after seeing Eric and imagining her new self. "Yeah, I'm gonna be confident because not one person on this side of planet earth can defeat me. Not one person," she continues spinning around in bliss at her new beginning until she stops, dropping to the ground at who she runs into right in front of her. "Dad!"

"Listen to Eric. I like him. He's good for you. I've been watching him."

"What? Daddy, I..."

"I know you love him. He loves you. I sat there in silence watching him in Tylon, and his concern is for you. He is continuing his duties as a Ty, and you listen to what he says. You may be stronger, but you aren't stronger than everything. You see what has happened to me. Go about your life carefully as if you have no powers, and my fangs will let you know when..." he says as he dissolves.

"Yes, sir. I love you, Daddy," she quickly states as she picks herself up from the floor. "You didn't have to scare me like that though. Thanks for stopping by and checking on me. Mom loves you, and she saw you but she didn't know it was really you. She knows about me, and will you come back and visit both of us at the same time the next time?" Her heart starts to swell, and before she knows it, she's back inside her bedroom crying for hours.

Chapter Eleven

In the middle of the night, Bailey lies in her bed wide awake with no way to contact Eric. She hasn't seen any enemy from Tylon again, and all she's been doing is sitting up waiting, trying to protect her mom and going without sleep, sleep that she thinks she needs but apparently not.

Although she cleaned herself up before her mother came home from work so that she wouldn't appear upset, as the night goes on, she continues to cry. There's such a heaviness on her chest, and she feels suffocated inside the house with no one to talk to about anything. She has no one. Her father is gone, and Eric can only come every now and then. She can't even get to Tylon without him, and if she does, is it even safe? Nowhere is safe for her, and she's slowly feeling trapped in a box.

Naturally, her instinct as a human being is to find a way out of any type of trap or captivity, and she can feel that hunger to free herself. She remembers as a child that her dad used to tell her that if you are ever cornered, fight your way out. Never sit there and not try to get away or take as many down as you can to get free. That's exactly how she feels now, and the feeling is strong.

She finally gets up from the bed, puts on her clothes, and decides to go into the front yard. She feels so shut in and surrounded by pressure that she may burst. Before leaving, she goes to check on her mother who is sleeping soundly in the bed, and then is certain that all the alarms are on the windows, then she leaves.

Immediately, the suffocation of the house departs, and a gust of night air brings her stress level down. Where it felt like she had a hard time even breathing, she now can expand her lungs. As she stands there on the porch, looking out in to the night, there is a sound behind her, like a click. She turns back toward the front door, but she sees nothing. Therefore, believing it was just a grasshopper or any other insect, she continues to relax and breathe in the comforts of outside. It feels so amazing, like she's never felt outside before. She feels like floating. She feels so free and light.

She looks up into the dark sky and smiles at the arrangement of stars twinkling above when suddenly the sound of peace changes.

"Nooooo! Leave me alone. Leave me alone! Bailey!"

"Mom?!" she spins around to open the front door, but it's locked. She bangs on the door as loud as she can. "Mom! Mama!!!" she calls, listening to her mother scream for help and as she prepares to kick in the door, she tastes blood inside her mouth and her fangs protrude from her gums while someone snatches her from the porch. "Mom!" she yells as her body is lifted into the air and slammed into the cement walkway. She gets back up, but every time she faces the direction of the attacker, the attacker is behind her. Therefore, instead of fighting she races toward her mother's window, and as she punches through it, causing the glass to shatter and her wrist to become streaked with blood, she immediately attempts to rip whatever is behind her with her fangs. There is success, however, in seconds, the arm that she's bitten down into throws her across the entire yard, slamming her into the street light pole.

As she attempts to get up, she's held to the ground, like something is wrapped around her body from the behind again, and as her mouth opens and fangs protrude, she is aware of something holding her neck against the pole so that she is unable to move it. Then, from the corner of her eye, she watches a long, knifelike nail slowly open the side of her throat about to slash through it when suddenly everything stops. She's loose, but when she tries to run, she can't.

Blood pours from the side of her neck like a fountain and the more she struggles to crawl toward her mother's bedroom window, the harder the struggle gets, so much so that she passes out on the grassy yard beneath the night sky. She lies there, seemingly all alone and unconscious, until she is taken away.

"She has to go to the hospital! Please, I need to call the ambulance! My daughter is dying! She's dying!"

"She won't die. Please, we can't let you do that. She will be fine. We must wait."

"Wait on what! Let me go!" Bailey's mother demands as a Ty holds her in place by her hand before she drops to the floor, weakened by the sight of Bailey lying there on the floor, blood all over the left side of her body.

There are at least five to ten Tys around and inside of the house, however, Bailey's mother only sees two, the one holding her hand and the other, an older Ty woman whom she doesn't know is Bailey's great aunt. Great aunt Baileen has her hand placed atop Bailey's deadly injury, and as she does, her hand pulsates and she breathes heavily, trying with all her might to take in as much oxygen as possible. It appears to everyone that she's keeping Bailey alive for as long as possible so that the blood that she spilled onto the ground can replenish itself in her body. While that's going on, those Tys on the outside are guarding and cleaning all the Bailey's bloodstains from the ground. No one can see them, especially in the middle of the night, due to their moving so fast. However, a light came on in the neighbor's home across the street when Bailey was screaming, but by the time she had awaken fully and gotten to the window to peep out, everything was clear, or as clear as she could see it. She even went to the front door and opened it to be certain, turning on her porch light, but she saw nothing. Therefore, she went back to bed, assuming the voice she heard calling was just a bad dream.

Finally, there's movement from Bailey's fingers, and her leg kicks as if she's still trying to fight someone off. Bailey's mother hollers her name as her great aunt stands and approaches her mother. "Who are you...and" she stammers, "what did you do to her? Why isn't she waking up? She's moving but she isn't answering me."

"The movement is all I need to see to make sure she will recover. They pierced her in her neck in a major vessel, and she would not have made it if we hadn't gotten here in time. Ericon, it's okay. She's fine. You can slow down now." As she speaks, an image is seen walking back and forth behind the couch. He had been there weeping, and as he comes into focus, the tears are still evident and his fists are clenched. "Calm, Ericon, and breathe. Take control back. She'll be here in a minute or two." Great aunt Baileen turns back to Bailey's mother. "I'm your daughter's aunt, and your husband's aunt. My name is Baileen. That would make you my niece as well. She lives, Lynette. Ericon will explain everything. We must go. We are sorry this happened. Remove yourself from her hand. Bailey is awake," she confirms without even looking back at Bailey as her eyes open. This startles Lynette, but she quickly snaps out of it and rushes to her daughter's aide. When she looks back, everyone is gone.

"Bailey, baby, Bailey, honey, wake up. Is she gonna talk, Eric? Bailey?" she continues, kissing her on her forehead, taking her daughter's hand into hers, stroking it softly while hoping to hear Bailey speak.

"She'll be able to talk any second now. She's healing rapidly. Her aunt … she's the one who gave her more strength. I'm sorry that I wasn't here on time. I got here as soon as I could," he continues as tears roll down his face. "They lured her out. I didn't even know. I don't understand..."

As he speaks, Bailey finally says something, taking her mother by surprise as Eric stands to turn away and wipe his eyes and regain a strong posture. "Mom? Where are they?" Although she just regained consciousness, her strength is like she was never near death. She sits up and places her arm around her mother, attempting to shield her from any attacks.

"No, Bailey, it's okay. No one is here. See, it's just me and Eric."

Bailey glances to her left to see Eric standing right beside her, but she notices that something's wrong. He's not saying anything, and his eyes look as if he had been crying. Then, she finally remembers. She remembers herself struggling to get to the window to save her mother before she remembers nothing. Bailey looks down at her hands and then reaches up at her neck where she was cut. There is no cut there. Finally, she glances back up at

Eric, remembering how he almost died but came back to life.

"Was I dying, Eric?"

A lone tear drifts down his cheek, and he can't make himself answer her. He has deep regret at getting here seconds after even her great aunt Baileen got there to fight for her. There were at least five Lonthians attacking her all at once, and they were strategic at doing it because they can't beat her alone, not on this side of earth.

"Eric!" she calls again, this time standing up, walking toward him and holding his hand. "Eric, tell me what happened. Mom?" she asks, turning to her mom. "It's okay. Just let me know."

"You were already dying when I got here," Eric chokes up. "They set us up. We were set up somehow, and I was...I wasn't able to get here because..."

Bailey's mom interjects, seeing how it's causing Eric extreme distress to tell her the story, "I met your aunt Baileen. She and some others were able to save your life, and Eric was here like seconds after. Your aunt did something to your neck, like healed it or something..."

"She gave some of her power to her. She had to be here to do it because it isn't her direct child but her niece. When enough power goes in, Bailey is able to heal on her own really fast. She won't ever need a doctor, not on this side, as long as we can get to her."

"And what if you can't get to me in time?"

The silence in the room is loud, and instead of Bailey feeling like she is untouchable, she suddenly feels more vulnerable and weak than she ever has in her life. When she was just a normal person, she was never in any fights and always felt safe. However, now that she's Black Fang, there's danger all around; it's like she's a magnet for it.

"Eric, answer me. What if you can't get to me in time?"

Eric stands there without responding as her mother walks up behind her, embracing her with all the protection she can give before prompting Eric to answer. "Eric, will you be able to get to her in time?

What's the window of time that you need to be here for my daughter?"

"This was the first time I didn't know that I wouldn't be the first one here. I'm sorry I failed you. I'm sorry I failed you both."

"But no, no, Eric," Bailey's mom replies. "You came. You came. You came with all the rest of them. I mean, I don't know what they all looked like or who they were, but you came, and we are both alive thanks to you and them. Without your relationship, who knows what would have happened to Bailey thus far. I thank you so much, and you don't have to feel bad. You're always welcome here. Always." She then reaches over to hug him tight, letting him know the sincerity of her words. As she hugs him, she can feel his heart pounding and his chest quivering, painfully holding in what to him was a defeat. Finally, she moves away and Bailey approaches.

"You were on time, Eric. You were on time for me. Remember that you were on time for me, and you always will be. I won't forget," she says, referring secretly about what happened in the alleyway between her and Delight. When she says it, he looks into her eyes, relieved that she still felt that she could trust him. She feels the burden of her life on his body, and she leans in and gives him a kiss on the cheek. From there, Eric doesn't say anything back due to the heavy amount of emotion overpowering his words, so he backs away and leaves. As he disappears, the words *"it won't happen again"* is all he left behind.

Chapter Twelve

"Come. Sit." The table is set with every dish that Eric has ever enjoyed since his childhood, and as he sat down, unlike normal, he doesn't have an appetite. His father sits down at the table and collects his food while his mother sits as well, however, she doesn't collect her food. Instead she keeps her eyes down while questioning Eric.

"Not hungry. I prepared this big meal for you and your father and you aren't accepting of it?"

"I'm accepting of it, but I'm not going to eat tonight." As Eric speaks, his father taps the table, disturbed by the blatant disrespect Eric is having toward his mother, prompting Eric to explain himself. "Somehow, Mom, you have been keeping me busy, busier than what I need to be. Dad isn't powerless. He still has power, power enough to do what he needs to do for the most part. He's a strong man, especially if he can do this much even after he did what he did for me. Now," he pauses, "I will always protect him. He is my father. I will always protect you, Mom. Always. But there is also someone I vow to always protect, and she lives on the other side. Not only that, there are other people who I lived with there, and if they ever get pulled into this, I will protect them as well. I won't tell you who they are, and you will never meet them, in particular you, Mom."

"That's enough!" Eric's father erupts, but Eric doesn't flinch though the strength of his father's voice vibrated through is body. In defiance, he held himself as still as he could, bracing himself internally as he feels his father's voice trying to break him into submission.

"Mom, I don't want to eat. I want you to tell me why you're trying to hurt Bailey." He turns to look at his father who has stopped chewing, and then he turns back to his mother who continues chewing and swallowing before answering.

"The question really should be why is she trying to get you killed?"

"She's not trying..."

"Don't tell me what she isn't trying to do! She did! Look at your father! Look at him now!" Eric looks and she continues, "Your protecting her is going to kill your father and more than likely you. I will have no one! No one left! This is not your fight!"

"And it's not for you to help her die!" Eric shouts back, stunning both his parents. "I flipped the walls because I had a funny feeling, like something dangerous was around, when I left home today. Oh, you must've forgotten this family can sense each other really well? Have you forgotten? Well, I flipped the walls just to be sure you were okay, and I saw you. Although my heart said there was danger, I was looking directly at you and you looked fine...even though you were speaking face to face with a Lonthian. Then, in seconds, that Lonthian was gone. Where did he go, Mom?" Eric asks knowing full well where he went.

"Eric, I sent you go get something that I needed, and that's all. You may have thought you saw what you saw but you didn't see anything. I don't consort with Lonthians. When have you ever seen me..."

" Today. I know what I saw, and then in the next second, he was gone. This was around the same time Bailey was attacked. It was the same time, Ma. I was gone. I thought that feeling of danger was about you, but when he left your presence and you seemed fine, I kept walking. As soon as I left, that's when that attack started, wasn't it? It was right after you were talking to them. Did you send me off on purpose? Do you want Bailey gone, Ma?"

"Speaking to me in this tone isn't good, Eric," she sighs. "As your mother, I can do as I please and if I wanted her gone, I would have killed her myself. I sent no one after her." Eric disappointingly stares at his mother and then at his father, who drops his eyes. That's when he knew that his mom's story is a lie. "Eat, Eric. If I wanted her dead, she would be dead. I don't want her dead."

"What do you want her?"

His mother doesn't answer. Instead, she continues eating as if all is fine, leaving Eric in a fit of rage and sorrow.

Eric doesn't rest that night or the next. He's constantly aware of all things around him, and his sole focus is Bailey. He even contacts Bailey's aunt, reminding her to let him know anything that's going on as soon as she finds out, whenever it has to do with an attack against Bailey. He falls short of telling Bailey's aunt about his mother's treachery.

In the middle of the night, Eric finds himself crossing over to the other side just to sit beneath Bailey's room window. As he sits, he recalls all the chaos that occurred in the very area where he sits, as well as the nightmare of Bailey having to be brought back to life. It pains him deeply, but he still doesn't understand how they were able to sneak up on Bailey like they did. How was she even outside when her mother was inside? None of these questions Eric had answered because he was too ashamed and just needed to get away from it, especially because he felt his mother helped set the entire attack up.

"Eric?"

Completely startled, Eric jumps up from the ground to find Bailey sliding her window up. She's in her pajamas, but just like Eric, she doesn't look like she's been sleeping.

"I see you aren't asleep either," he says kicking the grass before glancing back up at her. "I needed to come check on you, make sure you're okay. I'm sorry about..."

"Help me out," Bailey interrupts him, so that he can help her out of the window. Before her two feet even hit the ground, she starts to tell him not to apologize. "You don't ever have to do that. I know that you have and always will do what you can. Stop letting what happened bother you. It's not your fault. Honestly, it's my dad's fault. I inherited something that I don't fully understand, and I never should have even gone to Tylon."

"Bailey, if you can remember, what happened right before you were attacked, I need to know. I need to know how you were so caught off guard like that."

"Well," she starts, "it was a regular evening, but I can't say it was as regular as I wanted it to be. I felt alone, and I felt like I had no one. Then, I felt like I just needed some fresh air because I couldn't breathe from the anxiety of it all. My thoughts and everything were going everywhere, so..."

"Wait a minute. Are you saying that you couldn't breathe and needed some fresh air metaphorically or literally?"

Bailey, confused, answers him as best she can. "I think I was having an anxiety attack, so I felt like I really couldn't catch my breath. I felt like..."

"You couldn't breathe." He stares at her, and suddenly, Bailey remembers.

"You mean you think someone was starving me of air, don't you?" She recalls Delight and her powers of removing oxygen from her immediate area.

"That's what I'm saying. I'm saying that I don't think you were having an anxiety attack. I think you were being attacked and didn't know it far before the physical attack started. They were inside your house."

"What?" Bailey stammers. "What do you mean?"

"I mean just that. They were baiting you to leave the house, and you did, didn't you?"

"Yes."

"And then you couldn't get back inside?"

"No."

"Bailey, listen to me. They used your mother to get you. You're hard to defeat, so when you heard your mother being attacked, your focus left yourself and went to her. That's how they were able to…"

"Nearly take my life." Bailey shudders at the memory of herself losing all consciousness. "Or was I really dead, Eric?"

"I never asked your aunt. Only she knows for sure, and more than likely, she will always say no. If she didn't get here in time, you would have been." He reaches for her hand and caresses it softly.

"Bailey, I couldn't sleep. I needed to be here for you because...you're in more danger than what you know, and I'm sorry."

"Eric, what?" she asks as he clears the tears from his eyes. It hurts him to even think about what his mother has done, and he doesn't even think he can repeat it out loud.

"I wish I didn't have to tell you this, but I do, just so you know. Just in case she comes over to this side."

"She who?"

"My mother."

"What does your mom have to do with anything, Eric?"

"I should have never introduced you. I should have never taken you to my home. I didn't know."

"Eric what?" she asks impatiently, watching him nervously figit.

"She sent them. She helped them. She wants you not exist, and she wants you to not exist because of my love for you and your love for me. You're of duel heritage, Bailey, and that means that to her, you' re intruding on my destiny. She finally has me back, and the way she believes she can pull the strings is because she knows I love you."

"What are you saying, Eric?"

"I'm saying that I may have to never see you again in order to keep you safer than what you are now."

"How do you know your mother set me up?"

"I saw her with a Lonthian. The next thing you know, you were under attack, and I had no idea. She all but admitted it to me at dinner. She doesn't want me to return to you, and she's probably going to use your safety as leverage to keep me home, away from you, since she is now aware that I know what she did."

Bailey releases his hand but doesn't say a word. She doesn't know what to say. The woman whom she sat with in Tylon and took her to meet her flesh and blood aunt is now plotting against her, not just any plot, but for her death. Fear creeps around Bailey like a sheet, and her brown skin feels like it's turning as pale as the inside of a banana. Both Tylonthians and Lonthians are after her, and without Eric to let her know what's going on, she's all alone.

"I'm gonna die, Eric."

"No you won't," he affirms, reaching out for her again.

"Let me go!" she shouts before quieting again with tears in her eyes, looking directly into Eric's dark brown eyes. "Just let me go. If you let me go, your mom won't send them."

"They will come anyway, Bailey!" he stresses. "I just needed to let you know just in case she came herself, for the first time in her life to this side. You would then know and she wouldn't be able to trick you."

"Eric, what do I do? How do I protect my mom or myself? Why am I the most hated? Why is everything that's happening in Tylon and here have to do with me?" she struggles to understand. "I didn't do anything," she cries, finally allowing Eric to hold her in his arms. "All I did was exist. I shouldn't have to pay for the battles that my father had to face, especially one that he had to face because it was his job for the good of Tylon. The

Lonthians will hate me forever until they find me and kill me, won't they?"

"Your father killed one of their top. He was someone that they looked up to, but they won't kill you. If they come to kill you, they will have to kill me first. I'll let my mom know that as soon as I get back." Bailey moves back to make certain she is hearing him right. "It's the only way. I've been thinking about it, and in order to make her stand down, I have to tell her exactly that. She doesn't want me dead, and she will do anything to keep me alive – anything. Trust me, Bailey. She will back down. I love you."

"What are you saying?"

"I'm staying here. My dad will have to understand, and so will she. My staying in Tylon means your death, Bailey. My mom... I think she will eliminate you to keep me there with them. If she knows I will fight for you until my own death here, she will not only defend me, but you too, just to keep me alive. I've made my decision."

Bailey doesn't know what to say. She's never felt more protected since her father died, and she doesn't want to be left alone. At the same time, she doesn't want to be the reason Eric's family is torn apart. "I don't want anything to happen to you because of me."

"Something has already happened to me. It's the same thing that happened to your father when he met your mother. I can't change that. I'll never be able to change that. It's not the way of a Ty. Once we choose, we choose."

"Choose?"

"Who we love. I've always chosen you. I just had to wait."

"On what?"

"For you to accept your love for me. Now you do."

"How do you know?"

"Touch me here." He places her hand on his chest, and immediately, she it's like she placed her hand on her own. She quickly jumps back stunned, rubbing her chest frantically as he smiles. "I've been waiting on you to not fight how you feel or rationalize your way out of it. It feels good doesn't it? I choose you."

"I choose you, too."

From there, Eric rushes back to Tylon, leaving Bailey standing in front of her bedroom window with her hand on her chest, directly over her fang, before she hops back into her bedroom window and climbs into her bed in complete disbelief at her life and her love.

Chapter Thirteen

The next morning, Eric's mother walks into his room, seeing him lying there with eyes wide open. He notices her as well, but he doesn't acknowledge her at all. He stares up into the ceiling, preparing to tell her his plans. He'd been thinking of how he should tell her in order to make her understand fully just how serious he is. Knowing his mother and how she skillfully detects any hesitation in anyone at any time, he knows that he has to have full, unwavering confidence in what he's saying or she will call his bluff.

"You see me here, and I suppose you're still upset at me for upholding my duty to my family, not the family that you are trying to create with a half-breed. I don't have any allegiance to her love for you or your love for..."

"Which is why I'm leaving home and never returning. Since you have decided to turn your back on the family that I have *chosen*..."

"Chosen?"

"Yes, I don't just love her. I have chosen her. This is forever, mother, and you know that."

His mother laughs him to scorn, "She isn't Ty! She has no idea what that is and her belief is unlike ours. You will not have her for long, and definitely not until death. They leave each other time and time again there, and they have a whole set of rules. You have been away too long, Ericon."

"I have chosen her, and as you know, you, mother, don't have any say so over it. Also, mother," he states, getting up from his resting state, "I forbid you from approaching her in any way from this day forward. I'm leaving."

"Ericon, you aren't going anywhere."

"Watch me. Where's father?" he asks, not expecting an answer as he walks past her and out of his room. He finds his father sitting in the in his room on the floor as he normally does to conserve his energy. "Father?"

"I already know. I heard you, and you are right, son. Your mother was wrong. Go to whom you have chosen. I won't stand in your way, and I know you love me and your mother. Do not carry the guilt of me. Of all the things I give to you, I give you my life. I do not and will never give you guilt. Be the man that came from me. We will see each other. Forgive your mother. She misunderstands her love for you."

"Thank you, father." Eric falls to his knees and hugs his father tightly, promising to take care of himself and to never put his father in that situation again.

"No. It is my honor to give my life for yours. If I had to do it again, I would. Go. Protect her." As

Eric gets up, his father takes him by his wrist, looks him into his eyes and remains silent. He only stares, proud of him, before letting him go, only to see his mother standing there at the doorway again. This time, she has nothing to say, and instead of blocking the door to keep her son from leaving, she moves to the side and watches him pass without glancing at her at all.

Eric leaves Tylon but he doesn't go to Bailey's home. Instead, he went to his step-parents' home. They were sound asleep when he got there, so he walked inside the room and whispered for them to wake up. Startled by his voice, they both look up, shocked to see him back home, and immediately, they got up and gave him a huge hug. However, just like spies, they peeped around the corner and unplugged anything artificially intelligent and reassured him that they didn't tell anyone anything.

"We absolutely did not and will not, Eric. We don't know what made her stop by here but..."

"Wait who?"

"Bailey. The young lady you told us about. She stopped by looking for you in a frenzy the other day, and we didn't know she was one, too."

"She was one?" Eric repeats, partially grinning. "She's half Ty like me. I'm not an alien now that you know, Ma."

"Well, I didn't mean..."

"I know," he responds, and although he is happy to see them again, he can't shake the sadness he has after leaving his biological parents the way he did. "I just wanted to ask if I can continue to stay here. I plan on staying."

"Yes! Yes! Come on. Your room is just how you left it."

"Come on here, son. Glad to have you back. We can talk in the morning," his pseudo father chimes in, feeling proud that Eric rejoined the family, yet still very curious as to how things will operate now that he has knowledge of something so unfamiliar attached to his lifestyle. Although he's happy, he now wonders about so many unanswered questions, and his own discernment makes him feel like all isn't well. Yet, he keeps silent about it all.

They leave Eric to his room as they walk back down the hallway, excited to have him back, but as Eric lies down on the bed, he isn't as happy as his stepparents. He terribly sad, so sad, that he breaks down and cries all night long. The next morning when he awakens, his pseudo mother, whom he calls makes a big breakfast for him, and he meets both of them at the kitchen table.

They sit there with smiles on their faces as if Eric is a complete stranger. The chair is even pulled out, and as Eric sits, he notices that it's his favorite breakfast – eggs and sausage with a bagel with ginger tea and a glass of water. The first thing he touches is his glass of water, but they eye his hand and he pulls it back.

"Sorry," he says as they all bow their heads in prayer. When it's over, he then takes a sip of his water.

"Do you all have prayers in Tylon? We never asked because you seemed to know what to do..."

"Mike!" his wife exclaims.

"It's okay. It's okay. I am realizing that I look different to you, and that's because I am, but not by

126

much. I knew to pray because I've seen it before. We know you on this side much more than any of you know us. Some of us even try and do your dances," he laughs while taking the first bite of his bagel and eggs.

"You can see us from there?"

"No. Just hearsay from those of us who have been here and returned back over the course of time. That's all. Like there was this dance called The Worm and we still do that one because it really looks like a worm, but being over here, I know the dance is old now. They don't."

Instead of behaving like they normally would, they both sit there and watch as he eats his breakfast without touching their own much. Then, finally someone asks the question that he doesn't really want to answer.

"What made you come back here, Eric?" his Poppa Mike asks curiously as he wipes his mouth with the white cloth napkin beside him. "You were so adamant about leaving, like you had to and now you're back. It makes me wonder what's going on over there in Tylon that we don't know? I mean, should we be concerned?"

The question prompts Eric to stop eating. He didn't want any questions about the whole situation because he still hasn't processed it fully, so he doesn't know how to answer truthfully without terrifying them. Clearing his throat, however, he takes a shot at being as honest with him as he can. Mama Andrea notices his hesitation and sits up taller in her chair, believing that the question deserves an answer. They both notice how he appears this morning. His eyes are swollen, like he'd been crying all night. Last night, when they returned to bed, they sensed that something was the matter, almost ominous, so they decided to address it this morning over breakfast.

"To tell you the truth, I had to come back because I'm in love with the girl that came by – Bailey – and I won't let anything happen to her. I can't protect her from anything while I'm there, so that's why I decided to come back." Hoping that bit of truth would answer the question, he starts to eat again, and this time faster so that he can quickly leave the interrogation, but out comes another question.

"Protect her from what? I'm... we're glad to hear of your affection for her as she definitely has affection for you from what we saw, but why would she need protection? Is something going on that we don't know about that could potentially harm you?"

"Not many people harm me or her on this side," he pauses, "accept if they come over to this side as I am now, they could harm her because she doesn't know much about Tylon or those that live there."

"Why would they want to hurt her?" Mama Andrea asks concerned. "Couldn't they just as well hurt you?"

Before Eric could answer, Mike asks defensively, "Eric, are you telling us that we too are in danger? This all makes no sense. You're here to protect her, and right now we know as nothing but indeed it is something, and now that you live here with us again, are we in need of protection from whatever and whoever, too? Eric, I'm not from Tylon but I do understand the streets, and you're just as much a person as I am, regardless of your powers. The one thing about us is that when we suspect all isn't being told to us, it's normally the truth. Now, lay it out, Eric! I was once a young man, too, and there is a clear reason why things are happening, and we would like the clear answer. Please, son." he exclaims, losing patience.

Eric places his head into his hands as his elbows rest on the kitchen table. He's sure that he can trust them with his own life because they love him just that much and he can sense that all of this pushback is coming from a place of love and protection, for him and the family. He glances up at them with tears in his eyes, and then spills everything – how his mother and others are trying to harm Bailey and how her family has already been attacked and why he decided to live on this side for just that reason. The only thing he left out was how he nearly died during the death of Delight. That, he can never tell anyone because that would place them at the scene of a crime that no one on earth would understand had to happen. It would seal Bailey's fate as a murderer here and if she fled to Tylon, she would be surely killed.

"The safest place for her to be as a duel heritage is here, on this side because her powers are strongest here. As far as you and me, we are fine. You haven't offended anyone in Tylon, and no one even knows about you. You haven't stepped in on any lineage, and therefore, you will never be in danger. Just remain out of it, and nothing will ever happen. I mean it."

His pseudo parents sit there, not blinking and unable to eat another bite. Eric can tell that processing all that he'd stated would them some time, so he lifts his glass, finishes his drink and then heads out the door.

"I love you, too," he says with a smirk. "Stay safe. I'll be back soon. Thanks for breakfast. Don't stay there all day long now." When he walks out the door, he breathes in the day, feeling like he sat through a counseling session with a therapist and released all that burdened him. "Therapy really works!"

As he jogs down the steps, he doesn't reach the last step before noticing someone standing eerily across the wide road between both neighbor's houses. Eric questionably searches the area with his eyes only and then stares back at the person who stands in the shadows of the trees when suddenly, the person steps out into the light. Eric nearly takes a step backwards in shock, but instead, he plants his heel into the ground and pushes himself forward. Then he flips the scenery around to look behind the houses across the street, and what he sees terrifies him so much that he flips the scenery back. There are rows of Lonthians, and they stand in place waiting on orders by one of their leaders, Creytar.

Eric's pulse races, and his thoughts go back to the conversation that he had with his pseudo parents at the kitchen table. He told them that they wouldn't be in danger at all. He now knows that's a lie. Suddenly, a voice whispers in his ear, "Do you know where your father is, Ericon?"

Eric immediately turns to fight, but no one is behind him, and when he turns back around, everyone is gone. His pseudo parents step outside after noticing that he has stalled in front of the house oddly.

"Eric?" Mama Andrea asks. "Are you sure everything is okay?"

"Yeah," he responds, "but I have to go back home. It's my father." At that, he flees from their sight, and in almost an instant, he is at his parents' home again, searching for his father.

"Father! Father!" he calls, all around the home until he goes back outside to search, and that's where he finds his mother holding the head of his father in her lap as a crowd of onlookers guard them both. Everyone looks as if they had been in a battle. Their stances are perfectly aligned, and the outer band of the crowd faces away from his father, just like they are awaiting another attack. Eric's mother only stares back at him as he approaches his father who has moved on and will see them later.

As Eric leans over his father, his mother doesn't move. He then places his hands on his father's chest to release some power, but it isn't enough. He tries repeatedly but there isn't enough power to give back to his father who lies there waiting to return back to his physical form.

A rage enters Eric that he's never experienced before, and as he places his hands back atop his father's chest to try again, his mother speaks.

"You can never get angry enough to get him back. He is your elder. His power goes to you, not vice versa. He is your father. Wait on him. He will visit you. Now, leave him be. Go back to where you last were as it seems you prefer it – while we fight for you and your chosen – the two he gave his life for today."

"This is not my fault! You won't blame me for any of this! It's you!" Eric shouts, and those around him lose focus due to the accusation. At that moment, Eric's mother stands and moves toward him so that they are nose to nose.

"You should have been home this entire time because if you were, then your special chosen would have been dead and your father would have been still..."

"He *is* here! He is in his place of honor. It was his time and his honor! Unlike you, Mom. You have no honor." He then glances at everyone around him and then back at his only biological parent. "Do you, Mother?" he scolds her before walking around her. "Lift my father from this ground now," he demands those around. "She doesn't deserve to grieve as she has allowed him to rest on this ground longer than is accepted. He needs no cradle for his head. He needs a crown for this," Eric continues as his voice cracks slightly from the pain of speaking through agony, "I am his duty and honor, and he has done me and my family well."

As he walks away while the rest lift his father to the area in which Eric will choose for his father to lay, his mother doesn't move. Instead, she stands in all her rage while she delights in the emptiness to which no one else seems to be aware. The Lonthians are nowhere to be found. After such a fierce battle raged that took her husband's life, they have disappeared, and she knows exactly why her husband is gone, why they had to fight and where the Lonthians have fled to finish the job they started. To Eric's mother, Clivvanna, this is the revenge she wants and needs and for the first time in her life, she has a strong desire to join them in the task.

Finally, she walks slowly behind the crowd who believe that the fight is over. The Lonthians had come to kill who they targeted, so they have no idea what's going on. Clivvanna walks slowly behind as two Tys join her on each side. They appear confused at her demeanor but don't dare ask her anything. Noticing how her eyes are steadfast on her husband, they only remain in constant protection of her until and through the honor ceremony. Meanwhile, Eric speaks with only one at the front of the procession.

"What happened to my father? Who exactly destroyed his life?" Eric asks patiently as his rage grows more and more. He can focus on nothing else but complete revenge at who attacked his father.

"We don't know why he was attacked, but it came out of nowhere, Ericon. We fought off many, but I fear your father was too weak for Andragote. It was her."

Ericon stops in his tracks and the procession stops behind him. Then he responds, "Andragote?"

"Yes. And she said she wasn't done before she and others fled. We thought they were going to continue the attack but they didn't. Instead, look around Ericon. Just look? Did you not notice how empty?"

Immediately, Eric spins around, searching everywhere, until finally his mind resettles away from his father and the disagreement he had with his mother. He then remembers his father's blessing to the girl he chose, and finally, through all his pain and rage, he knows where the battle went in all his distraction. The battle went to Bailey.

Without anymore words, he walks to his father, kisses him, glances at his mother and flees to fight as his mother looks on and smiles.

Chapter Fourteen

"Mom?" Bailey calls as she enters the hallway after not hearing her mom at all leave the house. "Mom!" she sings as she peeps into the bathroom. "Mom, where are you?" She leaves the bedroom and goes into the kitchen before heading to he living room window. The car is still there. Confused, she slides on her slippers and goes outside on the front porch, but when she doesn't see her mom anywhere, she goes back inside. "Wait," she whispers to herself. "She must be out back." Since the back door is always key locked, she walks back outside the front door, heading toward the backyard.

"Mom? Aren't you going to work? I thought you'd left without saying anything, so..."

As she turns the corner, there's her mother, pinned to the tree by the finger of a being she's never seen before. The woman is tall and slender, long curly jet black hair and her veins pulsate so deeply that Bailey can see them from clear across the yard. She knows this isn't a regular human being. This woman is from Tylon.

Bailey bolts toward her mother, but she quickly stops at the sound of the strange woman's voice.

"Your mother will die, and she will die before your very eyes if you take another step. Then you will die. Shall we play this game?"

"Please, let my mother go. Who are you? I'm sorry. I'm only human, and I..." Bailey pleads.

"Only human? Is that all daughter of Yjotar?" she interrupts as Bailey watches her mother struggle to breathe due to the force being placed upon her neck. "You're not only human, Bailey. You're Tylonthian as well. Your father killed Xidon. He was our brother, *my* brother. Turns out, Xidon had a daughter. Did you know her?"

"Mom," Bailey whimpers, not wanting to reveal anything about the day that Delight was tragically killed by her own hands.

"Your mom can't talk and with just a little bit more pressure applied, she will die. Answer my question. Did you know Xidon's daughter. I ask because I never got a chance to meet her until after her death. I was shocked to know I had a niece. I

139

haven't seen her or Xidon since. You already lost your father. By any chance would you like to know what it feels like to lose your mother?"

Enraged, Bailey goes on the attack but is swiftly knocked off her feet, her body slamming onto the ground. The feeling that vibrates through her body feels like the grass beneath her his iron and it penetrated. Her whole spine feels broken as she tries to move but can't get up. As she lies there in pain struggling, she rubs her tongue across her teeth, but her fangs aren't coming down.

"Are you looking for your fangs, Bailey? You know, I used to know your father well. I'm going to remind you of something before you watch your mother die," she pauses. "Your fangs don't come out unless I'm about to kill you, no one else."

Andragote raises her arm into the air, grips Bailey's mother's throat, and as Bailey screams for the life of her mother, Andragote strikes, causing her mother to fall to the ground.

"Mom!" Bailey cries, but she quickly notices that her mother is okay. Her mother is crawling towards her, and there's another fight going on. It's Eric, and he's fighting Andragote!

"Can you get up? Come on. We have to go," her mother demands, trying to pick her up.

"You have to wait, Ma. I have to heal up and help Eric.

"I can't even see them, Bailey! How can you? All I can feel is..."

"He probably has a shield on us, so mom go back in the house. Hurry up. Get your car keys and drive off before the shield goes away."

"I'm not leaving you here!"

"If you don't, you and I will die for sure. I have to help Eric because if he dies, I die. Mom, go. Let me help us live. All I have to do is get close enough to her and my fangs will do the rest. Mom, I won't die."

"I love you, baby. I love you so much," she cries as she hugs her daughter gently. Bailey feels better and starts to stand up and her mother is stunned.

"Go, mom. I love you, too. We all die if I don't help Eric. Go."

As her mom flees, she concentrates until she can slow the movement of Eric and their enemy Andragote down. Before she gets a chance to locate them, several others appear out of nowhere in the yard, and when she turns around, she finds her mother stalled and in shock at what she sees appear before her like ghosts.

"Mom! Come back to me. Stand here. Hurry, mom!"

Lynette scurries back near her with her fists up ready to fight as Bailey calmly tells her, "Your fists won't work. Just stay behind me."

Immediately, several enemies charge Bailey at once and her fangs erupt through her gums, blood streaming down her chin more than it ever had. Each time her blood hits the ground, she senses a flurry of vibrations from each direction, and without thinking, her body reacts, striking and killing each enemy with her fangs. Her mom watches on as her daughter changes before her eyes, and she sees her baby girl take the life from other beings with her teeth, like her fangs are deadly swords, everything becomes too much as bodies drop in mid air at her feet, then out of nowhere, disappear. Confused and out of breath from the stress of the whole ordeal going on around her, she collapses onto the ground passed out. Meanwhile, Bailey continues fighting until none are left. Then she turns her attention to Andragote. The problem is that she doesn't see Eric, and from the way Andragote is looking, she can't seem to find him either.

"Looks like we're on our own now," she addresses Bailey. "You know, there's always a way to get you without triggering your fangs, Bailey. Guess what?"

Bailey doesn't answer. Instead, she steps in front of her mother, and is reminding herself not to move from her position of protection for the only one she has left on this earth.

"Well, since you won't answer, I'll tell you." Andragote
leaps forward and then quickly jumps back. "I know how to get around those fangs, Bailey," she sings. "And I'm gonna do it, too. Did your chosen leave you alone? Looks like he doesn't know how to be loyal like his dead father."

Immediately, Bailey is distracted by the news of Eric's father potentially being dead, and Andragote saw her flinch. This makes Andragote even more thirsty for blood, so she answers the flinch,

"Oh, you didn't know. He died today. And I killed him."

Both hurt and enraged that Eric's father is possibly dead, she impulsively moves forward to attack Andragote, but she remembers her mother and stands firm in her spot, protecting her mother.

"Eric!" Bailey hollers, tears rolling down her face, never taking her attention from Andragote. "Eric, where are you?!" Her veins pulsate, and her blood heats it drips to the ground from her gums.

"That angry, huh? Your father did that as well. We could all tell when he was enraged or not. He had to get that under control. It's never good to let your enemy knows how you feel, Bailey. We know how to use it against you. Here's a free piece of advice, not from your dear dead dad, but from me. Don't sit in your rage. Your fangs are less deadly!" she states as she unleashes a fierce attack upon Bailey who launches her most violent attack back. She's trying everything she can to, but she's noticing that what Andragote says about her fangs is right. Even though she comes super close to Andragote, her fangs don't have that same powerful pull on her as they did when she fought Delight. They seem slower despite the fact that Bailey is enraged.

Andragote releases a belt of laughter as she senses Bailey's confusion about the matter. "You don't' know that your body works in opposites. Surprise. If you get too hot, you freeze, and if you get too cold, you're hot. All of the women in your family are like that. That's why it pays to know them, which you don't. But wait! You met your aunt, and too bad she may die next."

Again, Andragote creates the worst attack against Bailey that she's ever felt, and this time, she feels she can't make it through. With every strike, she strikes her hardest to hurt Andragote but nothing is working. Who is this woman and what type of strange powers does she have that nothing harms her? Perplexed and slowly beginning to feel pains much deeper and at a more rapid speed, Bailey feels like giving up because though she's fighting her hardest, she isn't able to continue at this rate. She takes a quick second to glance out for help from Eric who is nowhere to be found, but when she glances back toward Andragote, the woman is less than two feet from her mother with her arm in the air in striking position. Instantly, Bailey throws her body atop her mother's as Andragote's full power comes down, but it doesn't reach her mother. Instead, it hits her devastatingly hard which creates a distressingly powerful eruption of her fangs, causing Bailey to in one bite, snap through Andragote's neck. Andragote instantly dies, and Bailey collapses on top of her mother. Everything goes black.

Chapter Fifteen

"I don't know! I don't know! She's not waking up, Eric! She's not..." Lynette breaks down, paralyzed in agony as she watches her baby girl not moving. Eric kneels over her very concerned as her Tylonthian great aunt wraps her in a special cloth and waits. "She's dying!"

At those words, Bailey's great aunt, Baileen, stands and places a finger over Lynette's mouth and wipes her tears. "Never say she's dying. She can hear you. She just can't respond. She can hear you and your pain she can feel. Give her your strength, what you call here, your faith, and we wait. She's healing. We wait, mother. Come with me."

Shaken by the aunt's words, she gets up, looks at Bailey once more as she lies on her bed and goes up the hallway, holding Baileen's hand. Lynette feels broken. She realizes that she passed out and left her daughter to fend alone and possibly is dying because of it.

"This isn't your fault. There is nothing that you can do or could do. Bailey is stronger than what you think. She's is very new to this life, but she's very strong. She's stronger than what she knows. We have been here before. The problem is that she hasn't been able to hone her skills and understand them fully. This is why I have chosen to remain here for one week. That is long as I can stay. I will need to teach her balance and focus."

"What if she dies?"

"Am I not planning her future with you? That thing, that faith I have heard you have. Use that. She will awaken. We wait. For some reason, your fear is your guide, and sadness is pulling you along with a tight grip. Those are the wrong guides at times like this. Have you not learned? They guide you into away from reality. I know about your God. Your daughter confirmed your God to me. Go to your God. He is wise I feel because He makes sense."

"I need to go to the bathroom. I need to go pray for my baby," Lynette answered, wiping her tears.

"Go, and we will be here. I will stand by the door. Tell Him I said hello when you see Him," she responds, not aware that He won't be seen when in conversation.

"It doesn't work like tha…" Lynette states, but quickly changes her tune. "Yes, yes, I will tell Him." Then she goes into the bathroom, shuts the door and prays.

"Thank you." Baileen stands there as she promised she would. "Maybe one day we can all sit down for tea and learn from Him. I would love to have him visit Tylon, and then we can all go visit Heaven for a walk through."

Lynette hears her, slightly confused, but she ignores her so that she can set her focus on her prayers to God, that He may be merciful to her daughter. As soon as she starts the prayer, not too long after she makes mention of Bailey, she hears her calling for her mother.

"Baby!" Lynette bursts through the door and into the bedroom where she watches Bailey sitting up but leaning on Eric. She runs over and takes Bailey into her arms and doesn't let her go, thanking

God for every single moment. That's when Baileen walks through the door with a big smile on her face.

"It's time to start, Bailey."

"Aunt Baileen? Start what?"

"Your training. We can't always be here, and Eric, he can't fight everyone all the time. He'll eventually lose, especially here. Therefore, since this is your side, you have a certain degree of advantage, or you should. Let's figure it out. Are you ready?"

"Yes," she states, kissing her mother as her mother looks on in awe as her child rises from the floor as if she wasn't near death. "Are you okay, Mom? I'm sorry about what happened, but it's over right now. Eric, will you stay with my mom?"

Her mother doesn't respond, but is in wonder and amazement as her baby girl is no longer behaving the same as she did prior to the attack. Lynette grabs Eric's hand, and he places his hand on her wrist, letting her know all is fine.

"She has to do this. She'll be fine. Her aunt will protect her." Then, he sincerely reassures her, "We will protect her, including her father."

Tears flow from Lynette's eyes, and as Eric looks up at the window while Baileen and Bailey pass by, Baileen nods her head in agreement with his decision. Lynette notices and asks, "What?"

"Like we sort of told you before, in Tylon, we die but we don't. It's the same here, but it's a bit different. Tylonthians, which is what I am and your husband is, we can still visit our loved ones, and not just our loved ones, everyone. We can visit. We talk and everything, but it's only for a short time and it can't be all the time."

"I remember you told me but why are you telling me this now?"

Eric then looks beyond her and into her dining room, causing Lynette to turn around. "He knew Bailey was in trouble. He came. There's Yjotar."

Lynette can't believe who she's seeing before her eyes. She turns back to Eric and then back to her husband who she thought was dead all this time. "Is it really you?"

"Yes, Lynette, it's me, and just like he said, my real name is Yjotar. I'm Yjotar from Tylon, and I love you still. You will always be my chosen."

"Yjotar," she responds, not certain if she's dreaming as she steps toward him. "That's different than Thomas, don't you think?" she smiles, her voice quivering, wanting to hold him, the closer she gets.

"Come closer before I have to go," he requests. "I want to feel you near me."

"You can feel me?"

"Yes. Just look into my eyes, Lynette. I'll never leave my family. I won't come always, but when there is danger, I will try and warn you somehow."

Lynette reaches out to touch him, but she feels nothing on her fingertips. This makes her shudder, and she pulls back but he lifts his hand towards her face in an attempt to wipe the tears from her eyes.

"I feel you. I feel you. You are my chosen. I will always feel you, Lynette. I will always feel you when I look into your eyes. You make me feel... alive... though I'm not dead. Don't be sad. Our daughter is strong. Eric is good. I've been watching him," he smiles, making Lynette feel more at ease. "I won't appear much more because I want to be able to when it's needed. She won't die. My aunt is one of the best. Tell my daughter I love her, and I also love you," he says before he disappears before her eyes. Lynette falls to her knees in agony, missing having the love and security of her husband by her side. Eric comes to her side.

"It's better for him to go. He won't be back unless he must. It takes his energy. My father just left hours ago, and I will never see him until he shows. I know your pain now, but we have to move on and live. They watch and hope for our lives, not our demise. Please, let me help you up, and until Bailey gets back, let's eat and I can show you what I know. Teach you something?"

Lynette smiles and gets up from the floor, answering, "Sure." She wipes her tears from her eyes, and Eric goes into her kitchen to pretend that he knows how to make more than grilled sandwiches and noodles.

Chapter Sixteen

For one full week, Bailey's aunt utilizes every second she can to teach Bailey everything she knew and more that she recalled from her father after watching him grow into the man he became - every detail about his life that she knew of, how he maneuvered around problems and how he even came to be one of the most skilled in Tylon.

Each day is a grueling workout, going from her normal one hundred jumping jacks to two thousand, twenty squats to leg presses by lying on the floor and pushing the couch toward the ceiling with her feet five hundred times. As Lynette goes to work as if all was normal, Bailey remains behind with her aunt. Eric remains with her mother, riding with her to work and meeting her after work. Each day was super hot, and Bailey learned how to keep her temperature stable no matter what the temperature outside.

"It's one of the most useful life skills you can have."

Bailey giggles, and her aunt looks up at her oddly and asks, "What's the giggle about?"

"I feel like a reptile or something. A life skill on how to keep my body temperature level?"

Her aunt smiles and proceeds to explain, "You already do this, Bailey. It's a life skill to know how to dress for the weather, isn't it? Just now, you can stand in the snow and not profusely sweat and attract attention while maintaining your power."

"You're right. I didn't think of it that way."

"We aren't too different, Bailey. Now...one other thing you have to learn is to not remain angry. You only have a short window to strike and persistent anger makes your natural attack weaker in rapid time. Therefore, learn how to be a tactical fighter, not an emotional one. The only sense you should have right now is danger. Allow that one. Nothing else. Once you can control your emotions, you will not be defeated."

"What do you mean? Do you want me to walk around like a zombie, Aunt Baileen?"

"Yes. If that's what it translates to, yes. Be a zombie. After you can successfully do that, bring the emotions back. You must know how to shut them down when fighting your enemy. They know you are a novice, and that you are different from them in several aspects. What is on your side is that you are stronger than most of them here. Never come to Tylon again. They will try to get to you, and if we can't protect you, they will kill you, Bailey. You have now taken the life of three of their own."

"Three?"

"Xidon...you inherit your father's past. Then you took Xidon's daughter and now Andragote. She was arrogant, believing that she could take your life here. Eric told me everything when he fled the fight to get us to come help. He is weaker here. Even you are stronger than him when you are here. The only thing he has over you is experience, and once you have it, you will be nearly invincible here. But once you gain the insight from me, you must use it. Your enemies are smart. They know ways in which to circumvent your deadly fangs. If Xidon's daughter knew how to, she would have probably killed you. You were both inexperienced, but it seems she knew much more than you."

"What if I need to come back to Tylon? What if..."

"You won't."

"But..."

"Don't!"

Bailey shuddered at her aunt demanding she stay away in such a forceful tone. She doesn't know how to respond back, so she just nods her head, pretending like she understands, but before she has a chance to walk away, her aunt takes her into her arms, hugging her tightly.

"Bailey, don't come back because I love you. You are the only duel heritage of our family, and I promised that I would watch after you. I promised. Help me to keep my promise. Look at me, and stop crying. Your father is gone out of Tylon. He isn't in Tylon. That won't make you closer to him. He only waits to see you thrive alive. Please, do not follow Eric back there ever, if he ever returns. Do you understand me? We will visit you and your mother, but don't speak to any of us Tys if Eric doesn't approve."

"Why?"

"You don't know who we all are. You want to be sure."

Bailey nods.

"Now, let's forget all about this stuff because it's making you fail."

"Fail?"

"You got sad. You're supposed to be a zombie."

"May I ask you a question?"

"I never said you couldn't."

"Has a Tylonthian ever attacked another Tylonthian or a duel heritage? I mean, is it normal?"

Aunt Baileen looks at her strangely, but answers. "I'm sure it has happened, but it's very abnormal. I've never heard of it because if Tylonthians attack to kill each other, that would mean they aren't Tylonthian. They are on the other side. What would make you ask?"

Her eyes shift, but she quickly stops them. "No reason to ask. I just need to know, just in case right?"

Her aunt remains quiet, but highly disturbed by her question because she can sense that something prompted her to ask, which wasn't out of simply curiosity. Instead of pushing the issue, she ponders it, pretending as if she discerned nothing.

"Well, since this is my last day here with you, I will say goodbye to your mother and you. Remember all I've taught you and continue to practice. Let no one see you practice the most important things, and also for the things that you will create naturally, strengthen them. They are what makes you unique, unlike any other Tylonthian or Lonthian. Right now, you are the only duel heritage that I know, and surely, you will develop skills that none of us have."

"I'll try."

"No. You will do. It's not a choice. It's not a try. It's an order, niece. Do it."

Bailey nods, still not as confident as she should be, but instead of continuing on in the conversation, they both go back to the house where Eric and Lynette have made a final other-dimension meal to send Aunt Baileen off.

"Soul food macaroni and cheese, cornbread and some beef ribs with..."

"A store bought sweet potato pie on the side because we didn't have enough time to make it," Eric adds.

"Well thank you all," she responds with delight. "Let's eat. So far, everything has been so tasty. This will be my first time tasting soul food macaroni and cheese. It's yellow."

"It's good. Forget the color. It's good," Eric emphasizes as he rushes and sits to eat while everyone giggles at his excitement.

As Baileen sits, she asks, "When is it that you finish school, Bailey?"

"In about three weeks," Bailey responds. "I'm not sure if I'm gonna walk or not...and when I say walk I mean the graduation ceremony. I ordered all my stuff, but..."

There is complete silence. Lynette cocks her eyes up from slicing the sweet potato pie and then looks back down as she continues to fraction it up. Eric isn't paying any attention to the conversation, too concerned with the food, while Aunt Baileen speaks on the situation.

"It's good that you won't go to the ceremony if it's just going to be you and your mother. I sense your mother's unhappiness of the situation because it's a big day. Therefore, if you go, then we will all go. You won't be there with all those Lonthians surrounding you."

"What? What do you mean?"

"They will come. If you go to the ceremony, more than likely they will be there. Will you make your decision now, please, the final one? Lynette?"

"She will go."

"Mom?"

"Yes, you will go. You've worked all this time for that special day, and I know you've lost much this year, but you will walk." She then glances at Baileen. "I know your family will try and protect you at all costs, just like I will. Therefore, you will walk, Bailey."

A smile erupts onto Bailey's face, and the entire mood turns into pure joy. For the moment, everything is calm and dramafree, something much needed when considering the disorder that has happened since the death of her father.

Chapter Seventeen

Graduation day comes with no problems. Life seems back to normal. Although Eric won't be graduating, he's happy for Bailey. There's no such thing as graduation from school in Tylon, so Eric doesn't feel pressed to do it at all. Instead, he lives through Bailey.

"Are you ready?" Bailey's mom asks as she exits the car with Bailey and Eric. Although Lynette is ecstatic for her only child to graduate from high school, she's still spooked by what could potentially happen during the graduation. Baileen's words about Lonthians being somewhere around terrifies her. Bailey can see that her mom is hiding her fears, so she speaks up.

"Mom, I'm your daughter, but I'm also the daughter of Yjotar. Just sit with Eric. The rest of my family will be here as well," she says, glancing at Eric, "whoever they are. My eyes will be on you, too, Mom, the whole time."

"It's gonna be fine, Mrs. Lynette. I will watch you and her at the same time, and if I sense one, I will let you know who they are to give you a sense of control in the matter, but you have to give me your word, you will do nothing or say nothing. Just enjoy the graduation."

"I understand."

"Now, let's not speak anymore about it because they can hear. That sense is far beyond yours, Mrs. Lynette, when it's activated."

"Can you do that, too, Bailey?" she asks, surprised.

"I'm not good at it, but I can. Let's go, Mom. Please listen to Eric, and don't forget to shout for me."

"And get put out?"

"I'm coming out anyway, so I'll meet y'all outside," Bailey laughs. "Just kidding. Don't leave me in there with those goons you think are coming, Eric."

"Shhh...let's just go."

The place is packed. The coliseum is huge, and people pile inside like ants. As she searches for her mother and Eric, she finds them sitting on the side the promised to sit, and then she starts to search for her aunt Baileen but she doesn't see her at all. As a matter of fact, she doesn't see any familiar faces from Tylon. Did they forget to come? Is something happening that she doesn't know about? Are the Lonthians here?

Suddenly, the ceremony starts, and Bailey stands with the rest of the senior class. She then rubs her tongue across her teeth in nervousness just to reassure herself that she's in no danger. Then she glances up at her mom, and there she is sitting there next to Eric, full of joy and snapping photos on her phone of her in the audience and of herself and Eric. Each time Bailey looks up, she shakes her head, giggling at her mother because she knows that if she doesn't stop videoing and snapping pics, her battery will run out at the most important part – the actual walk.

It isn't long before the speakers approach the podium, and then the valedictorian, but while Bailey sits listening, the valedictorian begins to discuss loosing a classmate, a classmate and friend to many, and a best friend to one – Delight. All the attention turns to a side screen with a picture and video of Delight, and not only Delight, but her in full joy with several classmates, including Bailey.

Why would they do this, Bailey thinks to herself as everyone beside her glances over and then begins to stand, applauding her. Horrified, she looks over at her mother and Eric confused, but they are sitting there normal as even the people around them are staring at her applauding. Confused and highly upset, Bailey stands and spins around at the entire crowd applauding her endlessly, and as she turns back again, she notices that the screen displaying the video of Delight's life in school continues to restart and play.

Terrified, she whispers repeatedly, "What's going on? What's going on?? Stop applauding. What's going on?"

"They called your name," someone answers her as they nudge her to walk to the stage.

Suddenly, Bailey snaps out of her daze and notices that she's already at the steps of the stage and everyone is waiting on her to walk across. Quickly, she climbs the steps and goes across the stage, but as she crosses, the entire coliseum is quiet except for Eric and her mother. No one applauds. It's silent except for the two people closest to her.

Bailey stops walking right before she is to take her diploma and looks around the coliseum for her Aunt Baileen. She scans intently until she finds her. She's standing inside on of the aisles, and she nods her head while pointing to the other side of the stage. Believing she's supposed to take that as direction, she continues across the stage, taking her diploma and then heading off the other end. As soon as her feet touch the other side, the eerie silence disappears, and all things go back to normal.

"Bailey!!" her mom screams which strangely catches her off guard. Bailey then looks up at her in the stands, flashes a big smile, poses so that everything appears normal as she tries to control her own special day, and walks on by them, waving with her diploma in hand. As she goes back to her seat, it's no longer there.

Trying once again to not attract attention, she peeps around and notices that the people in front and behind her are simply taking a seat, not even noticing that her chair isn't there. Therefore, she takes a deep breath, looks at the empty area beneath her and decides to sit – on nothing – hoping that it's just her imagination. It is.

After she sits, she looks down and to the side. Although she feels like she's sitting in the chair, the chair isn't there.

"I'm sitting on air," she states out loud, and the person next to her agrees, excited that she's finally graduated.

"Yes, I'm on cloud nine! Congratulations, classmate!"

"Congratulations," Bailey whispers as she looks behind her. No one behind her thinks it's odd for her to be sitting on an invisible chair except for her because they can see the chair apparently and she can't. Reaching down, she tries to feel what they can see, and she doesn't. There's just air. She glances up at Eric and he's peering down at her with an intensity that she's never seen before as her mother looks overtaken in a fit of clueless joy. Something isn't right she notices even more as Eric leaves his seat and moves forward, walking toward the balcony rails. She then glances over to where her Aunt Baileen was standing, and she's no longer there, and before she turns back to face the stage, a piece of paper lands in her lap. It's a note from Eric. She opens it to read, and it states to ignore everything. The Lonthians are sending her delusions, and he will alert her whenever something is real. No worries.

"Great," she rolls her eyes and then shuts them before looking back up to where Eric was standing at the balcony. He's there again, and no one around him even noticed he sped down into the graduates' section. He was just that fast. Meanwhile, Bailey grazes across her teeth to be certain she's safe, and she is, then she places her hand atop her chest, caressing her fang.

"I'm proud of you."

"Jesus!" she hollers, falling over into the person to her right.

"What? What's wrong?" the girl asks, checking around her. "Where is it? Is it a bug?"

"Yeah," Bailey lies. "It was big, too, but it flew away. It was one of those long legged, uh... daddy long legs spiders."

"Don't you just hate those?" the girl responds as she doesn't waste time screaming for one of her friends who crosses the stage dancing.

"Did you see the video?"

"What?" the girl asks Bailey confused.

"The video, with Delight?"

"Oh Delight, I feel so bad for her. Is there a video they're supposed to be showing?"

Bailey moves away. "No, no...I thought they would. Nevermind." Instead of sitting down any longer, Bailey gets up to leave without even looking up at her mother, Eric or anyone for that matter. She curiously turns back to look at her invisible chair. Just like she figured it would be – it's there. "I gotta get out of here. She waves her hand up to her mother and Eric, cuing them to meet her outside but as she approaches the double door exit from the auditorium, she sees her Aunt Baileen with her finger up to her mouth as she stands directly behind the officer.

As Bailey continues walking towards him, her aunt shakes her head and motions to her to go back and sit. The officer notices that Bailey appears confused, so he stops her.

"Graduation isn't over. Are you alright?"

"Uhh, yeah, yeah...I felt a little bit dizzy so I needed to get out of the crowd. Can I stand here for a minute?"

"Sure. Here, take my chair and have a seat. Congratulations on graduating. Any plans after today, college?"

Bailey notices Aunt Baileen warning her not to answer the question, and the officer looks behind him, kind of spooked out because he when he turns around to see who Bailey is looking at, he sees no one. She's there, but he doesn't see her. She's busy speed walking back and forth, leaving the officer blind to her presence.

"I don't have any plans yet. Just taking everything day by day, soaking it in."

"That's all you can do. Take things day by day. Would you like for me to grab you a drink, like a bottled water? You keep looking behind me..."

"Sure, but oh no...I'm not looking behind you. It's a technique I learned, focus on something in the distance to calm me down."

"Alright, alright, I'll be right back. Just right here around the corner."

As the officer leaves, Aunt Baileen shows up to her right. "Don't leave. Get the drink and go back to your seat. Don't worry about the hallucinations they are giving you. You're fine and all is well. Go back and sit down. Focus. You knew they would be here because I told you so. Now, that they have failed in making you walk out, they will probably stop for now. Go back."

"Here you are!" the officer says with a big smile on his face. "A gift from me to a new graduate."

"Thanks," Bailey nods as she opens the bottled water and takes a small sip. "Since sitting here for a minute, I feel better. I'm gonna go back to my seat."

"Go right ahead." The officer helps her up and watches her closely as she walks back to her seat, and as she looks back up toward her mother and Eric, they are both quiet and it appears as though Eric revealed what's going on. Her mother is squeezing his hand.

Eric notices Bailey looking up at him, and he nods his head, but as he does it, she tastes blood at her gum line. Instead of halting where she is, she continues to her seat as her Aunt Baileen advised her, and when she sat down along with her classmates, the blood inside her mouth disappeared. She looks back at the distance between her classmates and the officer, and it's a good distance. She then realizes that Lonthians were trying to attack her as she walked back because she was alone on that short walk. Out of curiosity, she looks up into the high ceiling and is stunned to the point of not breathing. They hover on the ceiling directly over her.

Now that her chair is visible again, she grabs the sides and secures herself to it so she won't run out again. Furiously, rubbing her tongue against her gums, there's no sign of imminent, life altering danger despite the Lonthians being directly above her head. Looking up again, they blend in perfectly with the color of the ceiling, and there are only a couple of them. She stops looking up, but instead, stands with the rest of her class, getting ready to toss up their caps. When they do, Bailey keeps her cap on. She stands there still in the middle of an erupting crowd terrified believing that at any point something could happen, not to her, but her mother or even Eric and her aunt as they try to defend her. She doesn't believe that she could even live with that, so when it becomes time to exit the coliseum, she doesn't stick around for hugs and pictures. She finds her mother and Eric and says, "Time to leave."

"You noticed them didn't you?" Eric sighs.

"You knew? You know the whole time that Lonthians were on the ceiling?"

"Yeah, I knew. But it's your graduation. Can't let them scare you," he grins. "Besides, they won't do much while you're surrounded in a crowd. The only time you were in danger was..."

"When I was walking back to my seat."

"Yes, but we had it covered."

"Mom, did you see them?"

"No, I didn't see a thing because I didn't even know," she answers looking around putting on a tough face for any and all enemies of her daughter. "Because if I did see them..."

"Mom! Just...let's go," Bailey interjects, smirking at Eric, as they know full well she hasn't a chance. She has the heart of a lion though, and Bailey knows that her mother will try and stop an eighteen wheeler truck for her. She means well, but really has no chance.

All the way home is a celebration. They left all of the other-dimension stuff that happened at the graduation behind so that Bailey could at least enjoy parts of her graduation day as a carefree graduate. They sing and dance in the car like they don't want the ride to end. Even when they arrive at the house, they ride on by it, deciding to not go inside and seclude themselves, but instead, go to a restaurant and arcade until the sun tells them to wrap it up and head back home.

"This is the most amazing day. Thanks for taking my mind off of everything."

"I told you that we would take care of you, didn't I? The key is to stay in a crowd. Lonthians aren't really for the attention. They're some major assassins, and what do assassins do?"

"They move covertly," Lynette answers. "They are covert, that's for sure."

"Which is why you really need to stay on guard whenever you're alone, okay? You and your mother. You all probably need to track each other with one of those things."

"Yeah, yeah...that's a good idea. Mom, do you think you can invest in those small trackers?"

"I will," she smiles. "I'll make that happen. Eric, thanks."

"It's my duty."

"Your duty?"

"Eric!" Bailey shrieks.

Eric continues speaking because he believes it's time for him to take everything to the next level. "It's my duty for someone whom I have chosen. In your world, it's the person whom I have chosen to be with forever. Will you accept this for us?"

"Eric!"

"Bailey, I already told you and my own parents that I have chosen you, and my dad who has gone on permitted me to continue on with you. He will meet with me soon I know. I would like to tell him about the confirmation."

"Confirmation? You mean wedding?"

"Oh brother..." Bailey sinks into her seat. "This is supposed to be my graduation day. Can we stay focused?"

"Yes, I agree, Eric," her mother laughs. "I think we should stay focused on graduation day, so talk to me about this in the morning. Let's go inside."

She pulls the car into the driveway, and they all get out, exhausted from such a long day. Every great moment squeezed from it was well worth it, and now they drag to the front door, go inside and change clothes to settle in for the evening. As soon as everyone gets changed, the doorbell rings.

"Are you expecting someone, Bailey?" her mom calls from her bedroom.

"No... no. Are you, Eric?" Bailey asks walking out of her bedroom into the living room where Eric is already sitting in front of the television for the night.

"I wouldn't invite anyone over here, Bailey," he says without looking away from the television. "It's a lady though. I don't know who she is, but she's out there, holding what looks like a cake."

"Really?" Bailey asks confused.

"Yeah, peep out the peephole. She looks safe. She's just standing there. She's not a Lonthian."

Bailey walks over and peeps out, then she steps back, glances at Eric who isn't paying attention to her, and quickly decides to just open the door without saying another word. She doesn't want him to know who it is, so she only addresses her with a warm greeting with no name.

"Hi! Come in!"

"Thank you, Bailey. I just...just wanted to uh...bring you a cake and celebrate since I have no..."

"Sure," Bailey cuts her off so Eric won't hear anymore.

"Oh, hello, my goodness. Come on inside," Lynette says entering the living room. "Please, come inside. And bless you, oh my!" Lynette continues as she takes the pound cake from the woman's hands and leads her to the kitchen table. "Bailey, go get us some plates and pour us some drinks. Sit down, sit down. You're always welcome here."

"Am I?" the woman asks.

"Yes, of course. Delight was like a sister to Bailey, and because of that, she was like a daughter to me. Just the loss alone for you..."

Immediately, Bailey brings the plates out with utensils, places them on the table and stares over at the back of Eric's head, and she clearly sees him no longer staring at the television, but staring straight ahead, over the television. As she's watching his neck tense up and him stand up from the sofa, he slowly turns and walks down the hall.

Quickly, she then turns to grab some drinks then she slams them on the table accidently as she's in a rush to go into the hallway with Eric.

"Bailey! What's that about? Slamming…"

"No ma'am. I really have to go to the bathroom."

Delight's mother grabs her by the wrist. "Hurry back. I want to celebrate with you, since Delight would have it no other way." Then she turns back to Bailey's mom as Bailey scurries down the hallway. "I was at the graduation you know. Bailey seemed deep in thought."

"Yes, well, she's had a rough time, losing her father and her best friend."

"Her sister. Does she speak about her much?"

"Well…"

As they speak, Eric reaches over and snatches her quicker into the hallway. "You didn't tell me that was her mom!" he strains quietly.

"I know. I felt my gums. They aren't bleeding, and she isn't Lonthian. How much danger could she possibly bring to me right now? I mean, she's in my house. I'm not in hers."

They both stand there quiet before thinking.

"The cake," they say simultaneously.

"Wait, Eric," she grabs him before he walks out there. "Wouldn't I have felt something in my mouth?"

"No. You haven't tried eating it yet."

"Mom, mom," Bailey states, rushing out past Eric who is right behind her. "Yeah, mom, I ..."

"Bailey, what is wrong with you? Don't interrupt her when she's speaking."

"I'm sorry, Ma, but let's not eat it right now. It will be better if we go to the..."

"Go where? What is wrong with you? You love pound cake, and I already tasted it. It's good," she says, slicing another piece and handing it to Bailey. Bailey doesn't reach for it at all. Instead, she rolls her tongue over her fangs and feels nothing. She then quickly looks over at Eric who is at a loss for words but staring hard at Delight's mom.

"You already cut it? Without me?" She takes it from her mother and inspects her for illness. "I see. And I bet it's good huh? So you already tasted it?"

"Just a small bite. It's good," Lynette answers, slightly embarrassed by how Bailey is behaving. "Don't be rude, Bailey. What's going on with you?"

"Yeah well she's not eating it."

"What? Eric!" Lynette shouts appalled.

"Mom..."Bailey interrupts. "Mom, just..."

"Bailey, now you listen to me."

"Why don't you want the cake, Bailey?" Delight's mother asks with a full smile on her face as she sits cross legged in the chair. "Do you think it's poisoned?"

"Excuse me?" Lynette says, now turning her attention to Delight's mother. "Poisoned? Why would you say that?"

"I'm asking your daughter a question," she continues, this time standing up, approaching Bailey slowly with that same eerie smile. "Do you, Bailey? Do you think I poisoned your poor mother?"

"What?" Lynette says confused, rubbing her throat while seeming to have a panic attack.

"Mom, go throw up. Do it now." Bailey says as she rubs her tongue across her fangs. Still nothing, and she motions to Eric that she isn't in danger by waving him away.

"If it's one thing you don't know, Lynette, it's your daughter. She isn't who she says she is, does she?"

"What are you talking about?"

"Your daughter here caused me the most pain that I've ever felt in my life. I figured everything out."

"Did you figure everything out? Or did someone pay you a visit?" Eric asks.

"Mom?" Bailey calls as notices her mom breathing much deeper and heavier than normal. "Mom, are you okay?" She then looks down at the slice of cake belonging to Delight's mom. She didn't have a piece. "Mom, go to the bathroom. Go vomit. Go!"

Lynette stares in deep confusion at Delight's mother. "You poisoned me?"

"Your daughter killed mine."

Lynette falls back against the wall, stunned at the revelation, and Eric catches her before she hits the floor. As she squeezes Eric's arm, she orders Delight's mom to leave.

"Get out of my house," Lynette struggles before taking a deeper breath and shouting, "Get out of my house! Now!"

"I sure will, and it looks like you will be leaving your home, too," she answers, not taking her eyes off of Bailey. "Now, Bailey, harm me. Go ahead. What I learned is that I can take the life of anyone except for you, and I did. Watch her die."

Bailey furiously lifts her hand to strike, but Eric quickly grabs her arm, barely able to hold on. "No! She will die from your strike, and she wants you to be arrested. Her death will happen here, in your house, by your own hands! We need to get your mom some help, now!"

Delight's mom laughs hysterically, and she doesn't move from her spot watching Bailey's mother gasp for breath as Eric restrains Bailey from killing Delight's mother.

Bailey then immediately turns to her dying mother who still gasps for breath. "Eric, I need to get my mom to the hospital now! Lift her and take her there fast. Hide us like you did with me in the alley! She's dying!"

As Delight's mom stands there laughing, another force enters the room out of nowhere, and blood enters Bailey's mouth. "Eric! What's going on? I'm in danger!"

Eric flips his vision to the outside of the house and sees no one, but because Bailey's fangs are beginning to protrude, Eric jumps in front of her and her mother, and as he does, he's knocked to the other side of the room. He immediately rises back from the floor, and that's when he sees him. It's Delight's father.

"Bailey, grab your mother and go! He's over you!" Eric then leaps forward, blocking the power of Delight's father from Bailey as they escape the house with her mother, ending up at the hospital in less than two minutes.

Chapter Eighteen

"My mom. She's been poisoned! Please help her. She isn't breathing. She's struggling!" Bailey cries, watching her mother fight for her life. She turns to Eric. "Can you go get my aunt?"

"She already knows. She should anyway. She can see your distress, remember. I just don't think she has power over your mother like she does over you." Eric starts to glancing about around the area to be sure they're safe. "We're in the right place. Follow your mom, and stay as close to her as you can. I'll stay out here. Go!"

Bailey remains by her mother's side as they wheel her back through the double doors to rush her into treatment to hopefully save her life. It's when Bailey refuses to leave her mother's side that they sit her near the door in the hallway allowing her to stay near as long as she doesn't interrupt and remain calm, understanding that it's her only parent and that she has no one else, including that it's on her graduation day.

"I know your face, from the school. You may know my daughter," says the nurse, pulling out her cell phone to show Bailey. "This is my little LahLah. Her name is..."

"LaNeethia. I know her," Bailey answers with a slight smile. "She's smart. She was in my math class."

"Thank you. She can't wait to graduate next year, like you." She reaches over and touches Bailey's hand. "Your mom will be fine. She will be fine. I'm not supposed to say anything, but by the looks of it, you got her here just in time. I've seen people who don't look half as strong as your mother make it, and I'm telling you that she will be fine. Believe me. You will, too."

Bailey watches her get up and walk into a patient's room, and as she sits there painfully waiting on word about her mother, she notices her father sit beside her. No one seems to see him but her, but she doesn't budge. Instead, she whispers.

"Delight's mom did it. I'm sorry for being so stupid." The worst guilt races through her heart and down her face in the form of tears. "I don't understand…I just don't understand, Daddy. I'm so sorry."

"You won't ever make that mistake again. You needed this. Look up." Then he disappears, and as she looks up, someone is approaching. She stands.

"I want to go see my mom."

"Good because she's okay. Come on. She wants to see you, too."

Bailey doesn't wait for him to finish. She's already walking into the room, and when she lays eyes on her mother, she rushes to hug her and her mother the same. They embrace each other like they haven't seen each other in ages.

"Dad came."

"I know. I know he would have come to be by your side. Where's Eric?"

"He's out front. You want me to get him?"

"No, no…just tell him I said thank you. I don't think they will let him back here. I'm surprised they let you."

"One of the nurses knew me and felt bad for me, so I think she pulled some strings. Mom, I'm sorry. I was stupid to…"

"Is it true?"

Bailey backs away, terrified at her mother's question. She doesn't want to answer, but she also thinks her mother will understand now that she knows so much more than she would have known at the time of the death.

Instead of saying anything out loud, she looks around and then nods her head. Then her mother speaks up quickly.

"We'll talk when we get back home. They say I will be able to leave later. It was poison," she stalls, "And now I know why."

Eric's pseudo parents come to pick them up in their SUV, and they all go home. Inside the car is silence, and when Bailey looks at the Eric's mom, Andrea, her face is stone. She appears almost scared to death, and Bailey has no idea what she knows because Eric hasn't had a chance to tell her. Therefore, as Lynette rests her head on a soft small pillow that Andrea brought from the house, Bailey taps Eric on the leg then she mouths *tell me* before handing him her phone. He then starts pecking away.

When I called Mom, she was wondering why I was calling from the hospital. She thought I was hurt, but when I told her that I needed a ride, not just me but us, she started asking what happened? I was about to hang up and just speed her back to the house like we got her here, but I didn't want to just do that. Instead I wanted everything to feel normal for her because she almost died. Anyway, so I told her. I told her everything that happened today, so that's why she's sitting there quiet. It's called digestion. They know everything, and when I say everything – everything except about ... you know.

Bailey is relieved when she reads that the everything doesn't include her taking the life of her best friend, and as she is taking a sigh of relief, Eric snatches the phone once again.

And they don't know who poisoned your mom. I just said she was poisoned, and I blamed it on Lonthians. I'm hoping they won't ask your mom anything about who did it.

He hands the cell phone back, and Bailey nods as the car pulls up to their house and they all exit the vehicle. Then, outside comes Mrs. Conyers, sliding across the street as quickly as she can in her house shoes. The sun is already down, and she looks like she's super excited about something but no one knows what.

"Lynette! Lynette! Somebody was in your house. It was a woman, and she...well...I never saw her before but it looks like she damaged your house really bad. And she kinda scared me when she left me a message to give to you, and that's why I'm out here now. She said to tell her to *send my son home or you will find worse soon enough.* Now I tried to tell her that you had a daughter and ..."

"Thank you, Mrs. Conyers. I just got in from the hospital because I wasn't feeling well. I will talk to you tomorrow.

"But, Lynette, I think it's bad in there," she warns, backing away from the driveway. "I just wanted to mind my business when I saw..."

"Bad? In my house?" Lynette asks stunned.

"Wait, let me go inside first," Eric states as he moves forward, Bailey moving right behind him.

"I'm going," she says, grabbing Eric by the wrist. "I know when I'm in serious danger, and it's my house. Eric, please stay here and watch them. Remember how they like to isolate us. Well, protect them, and I can protect myself." She looks at her mother. "Trust me, mom. I'm no longer afraid."

She moves forward, unafraid and angry. Flashes of her mother dying before her very eyes and remembering how this isn't the first time she's been targeted, Bailey walks into the house knowing that whoever is waiting, she will kill. The old Bailey is gone. She feels nothing as she continues walking inside the home she grew up in with her loving mother and father.

The house is torn to pieces internally. Not only is the floor still messed up from when Bailey was attacked and dragged, but there's more stuff that has been destroyed, from the furniture to the walls and the ceiling. The ceiling has been clawed from one area to the other, and the dining room table where the poisoned cake was located is all in pieces. And as Bailey moves forward, her mouth is filling with blood.

Instead of backing away like she normally would, she moves forward. The fang inside her chest throbs, and the more it throbs, the angrier she gets, the less she cares. If there are people trying to kill her, then she has to defend herself. Suddenly, she hears her Aunt Baileen's voice in her right ear.

"You are not a murderer. You are a defender – a defender of your family and friends. Now look to your left and destroy her."

Immediately, Bailey looks into her mother's bedroom and strikes. Again, her Aunt Baileen, in a faint call says, "Left strike again and kill! Do it now!"

Bailey strikes and suddenly, her fangs rip through the flesh of a Lonthian who leans backwards and appears as clear as day. It's Eric's mother. Bailey's fangs loose her and she drops to the floor, and as she drops, the smile never leaves her face as she says, "Now he will always regret he chose you, and he will never choose you again."

Devastated, Bailey falls back against the bedroom door, staring at Eric's mother dying before her very eyes. Then she scrambles up, her thoughts full of confusion and fear, fleeing to the driveway where everyone waits for her including Eric.

"Eric, come! You have to come! I'm sorry. I'm so sorry! I didn't mean it, I didn't..."

Immediately, Eric glances over at Bailey, and with the energy that she gives off along with her apology, doom overwhelms Eric to the point that he rushes in the home, trying to ignore the feelings that are entering his system at once. It takes him no time to find his mother, and when he does, he falls down at her side and remains completely silent. Bailey walks inside the room. He doesn't look up.

"I couldn't see her, Eric. I couldn't see her until after. I thought someone was here to kill me, and my fangs...I didn't know. I would have never. I didn't do it on purpose, and you know I couldn't have ever done it on purpose."

Eric refuses to look up at Bailey. Instead, he takes his mother into his arms and tries desperately to send her enough of his strength to recover, but no matter how hard he tries, nothing works. In reality, he knew it would never work, but it was the only thing that could soothe him as his own emotional stamina began to diminish while he even began to severely doubt who he chose.

Without speaking, he lifts his mother and faces Bailey. She then stares back at him, ashamed of herself and her own power, almost hating her own self. Tears flow, but she can sense that Eric remains unmoved. He stands there expressionless, wanting to leave, and there before her very eyes, he disappears, taking his mother back to Tylon himself.

To her knees, Bailey falls, emotionally unable to gain any composure until she hears her aunt's voice again.

"Stand. Clean up now. Use your speed. Hurry."

Wiping her face, she jumps up and within two minutes, everything is clean in her mother's bedroom, and as soon as she finishes, that's when

Eric's pseudo dad enters cautiously as if he's ready to attack to defend not only Eric, but everyone. Mrs. Conyers hastily scurries back to her house, completely afraid, and soon after Mrs. Conyers enters her home, Bailey hears police sirens from miles away.

"Eric is gone. He had to go back to Tylon. Right now the police are on the way. None of us were here, so we don't know who or what happened. I don't either. If you attempt to say anything else, no one will believe you."

"I saw blood on you when you came outside," Eric's pseudo mom stammers. "Where's Eric again?"

"He's back in Tylon. He's not here. You can check one thousand times, and you won't find him in here. You all know enough, and now we have to remain normal when the cops get here. Mom, sit down. You probably want to leave," she says turning her attention to Eric's pseudo parents."Eric will probably contact you soon."

They both agree and then leave before the police get to the home, leaving Bailey sobbing in her mother's arms.

"Mom, I'm so sorry!"

"What, baby, what? Stop crying. We can get more stuff," she explains, consoling her daughter.

"No, Ma, no… I'm not the same. I'll never be the same. They're dead because of me! They're both dead!"

In Tylon, Eric leads the procession for his mother as everyone crowds him asking him what happened to her on the other side. He doesn't mumble one word. Instead, he watches the crowd continues to grow while they murmur about revenge against the Lonthians for what they have done to her as they did to his father. In the midst of all the murmuring, he locks eyes with Bailey's Aunt Baileen, and neither one break their stare.

THE END

BLACK FANG 2